POISONS, POTIONS, AND PARASOLS

A PADDY'S PEELERS MYSTERY

BOOK THREE

AUBREY WYNNE

PLATO PUBLISHING

ISBN: 978-1-946560-51-3

Editing by The Editing Hall
Paddy's Peelers Logo Art by Jaycee DeLorenzo

🌸 Created with Vellum

POISONS, POTIONS, AND PARASOLS SUMMARY

She's content with her life...

Miss Eugenia Chapelle was born on the wrong side of the blanket. After her mother was disowned and fled to London, she pretended to be the widow of a French aristocrat to draw customers as a modiste. After her mother's death, Genie continues the lie, playing the half-French designer of Madame Chapelle's and running the business with her aunt. She never expects an earl to search out his illegitimate daughter twenty-six years later.

He will rip it apart...

Mr. Clayton Pierce works for one of London's most respected investigators. He has two cases on his docket—tracking a gang of counterfeiters passing banknotes and finding a long-lost child of an earl. When he meets the beautiful and talented Miss Chapelle, his attraction for her is as strong as his obsession with solving mysteries and catching criminals.

After Genie witnesses a possible murder at Hyde Park, she becomes a key witness in his first case. Then, by a twist of fate, she also becomes linked to his second assignment. With danger lurking around every dark corner, and the past the murkiest shadow of all, Clayton learns that solving a case does not always guarantee satisfaction of a job well done. As passions flare and the stakes are raised, will his success as an investigator be his ruin in love?

Set in the hectic district of Cheapside during the Regency, Paddy's Peelers search the dregs of London with skill and cunning to bring criminals to justice and, perhaps, unexpectedly find love along the way. A sweet but action-packed romance.

THE STORY OF PADDY'S PEELERS

The Story of Paddy's Peelers

peeler, *n.* 1816

...Originally: a member of the Irish constabulary. Later: (more *gen.*) a police officer; *spec.* a member of the original London Metropolitan force...

Patrick O'Brien, previously of the Dublin Police Force, left Ireland with his wife Margaret and arrived in London in 1798. Paddy was frustrated with both the lack of government involvement in fighting crime and the unreliable pay received by officers. He wanted to belong to an organized body of policing.

Margaret's stepbrother worked as a Bow Street Runner, and this new policing force greatly interested O'Brien. Housed at 4 Bow Street, it was directly attached to the magistrates and court and received some funds from the central government through grants. The Runners were to become the model of the future, proving to the government and the public that a professional police force could reduce crime.

O'Brien soon gained a reputation at the Bow Street court for his clever and expedient investigations. While his professional life provided him great satisfaction, his personal life was lacking. Paddy and his wife lamented the absence of children in their household.

When Paddy stumbled across a sick waif in a rookery alley, he brought the lad home. Over the next ten years, their "family" grew to a brood of seven. The couple developed the unique talents of their six boys and one girl. As the children grew into adulthood, O'Brien created an agency which utilized the skills of his brood. All the men spent an allotted time as a constable for Bow Street, learning the trade from seasoned Runners while working in the "family business."

Nicknamed Paddy's Peelers (*peeler* being slang for an Irish policeman), O'Brien's crew became an efficient team that included investigators, a physician who doubled as a coroner for autopsies, a solicitor who specialized in criminal law, a female master of disguise able to infiltrate any level of society, and a barrister who later joined their ranks to present certain cases pro bono in High Court.

Set in the hectic district of Cheapside during the Regency, the O'Brien clan search the dregs of London with skill and cunning to bring criminals to justice and, perhaps, unexpectedly find love along the way.

SERIES LIST

Paddy's Peelers Mystery (Historical Romantic Suspense)
Sweet romance,
Crimes, Conspiracies, and Courtship
Pads, Purses, and Plum Pudding
Poisons, Potions, and Parasols

Once Upon a Widow (sweet Regency)
Earl of Sunderland
A Wicked Earl's Widow
Rhapsody and Rebellion
Earl of Darby
Earl of Brecken
Earl of Griffith
Beware a Wallflower's Wrath
A Wallflower's Wassail Punch
A Scoundrel's Christmas Challenge
The Duplicate Duke
Kiss the Scoundrel Farewell

PROLOGUE

Spring 1803
Whitechapel, London

*M*argaret O'Brien made her way down the dim hallway, avoiding the walls desperately in need of another coat of whitewash. She paused before a door cracked partway open.

"NO!" cried a boy's frantic voice.

"She's been gone awhile, Clayton. I'll have to send word and hope someone comes by to pick her up today."

Maggie recognized the landlady's voice, and a chill ran through her. Her friend had been ill, just a slight fever. They'd both assumed it was only a chill from the rainy spring weather. She had dropped off some food for Edith's son a few days ago and had decided to stop by and check on the pair. She pushed open the door and drew in a breath.

Edith's son, Clayton, was on his knees beside his mother's bed, arms spread across her still body. "She's just sleepin' I'm tellin' ye. She's so tired. It'll be fine, Mrs. Ober. You'll see. She'll wake up and be fine." He buried his face in the thin blanket covering his mother, his auburn curls shaking with his sobs. "She'll wake up soon. I promise."

Mrs. Ober gave a loud sigh. "Clay," she said in a softer tone. "Your mother's dead. She can't stay here anymore. And neither can you." She laid a hand on the boy's shoulder, and he shrugged her hand off with ferocity.

Maggie blinked back tears and rushed forward. "Hello, Mrs. Ober. Would ye mind if I tried?"

The landlady's tired eyes shone with sorrow and gratitude. "Ah, Mrs. O'Brien. He's a good boy on most days. This took us all by surprise," she said in a hushed voice. "He couldn't wake her last night. Hasn't left her side since. Been wiping her with a wet cloth most of the night I imagine."

Bending down near the boy, Maggie picked up the bowl and rag and handed it to Mrs. Ober. "Could ye get rid of dis for us?"

The woman nodded. "I've been trying to get him out of here. It ain't natural—"

"To lose yer mother when ye're nine years old," finished Maggie. She fished in her reticule and pulled out a few coins. "Send for da undertaker. I'll pay for a coffin to be rented so she gets a burial. And I'll see to da boyo."

Mrs. Ober nodded, her mobcap sliding back on her gray curls. "Thank ye, ma'am. You're right kind, ye are."

When the door closed with a quiet *click*, Maggie looked around the room. A rocker by the small coal stove. One wobbly table and two wooden chairs. With a deep breath and an even deeper determination, she pulled one of the chairs over to the bed and sat next to the boy.

"Clayton," she said quietly, stroking the boy's riotous curls. "Yer ma is no longer hurtin'. She's gone to a better place now. We have to take comfort in dat."

He sniffed and nodded his head but didn't lift his face from the blanket. "If I leave, then she's truly gone. I'll be alone. All al—" His voice cracked, and the thin shoulders shook again.

Maggie leaned down and wrapped her arms around him. "Nay, boyo. I'm here. I won't leave ye alone. Now, let's say a prayer and give yer ma a proper goodbye. I t'ink it's what she'd want."

After what seemed an eternity, the boy sat up. His sea-green eyes were swollen, his cheeks tearstained, but he lifted his chin with courage. "How do we do that? Say goodbye?" he asked.

"My da always said memories were like epitaphs. In Ireland, we talk of da best of someone's life to remember them by. Tell me one of yer favorite t'ings about yer mother." With gentle fingers, she pushed his damp curls away from his face. His skin was hot, and she worried he might be coming down with whatever fever his mother had caught.

"She has the voice of an angel. She sings to me all the time." He sniffed and swiped at his cheeks. "I'll never hear her again."

"Aye, ye will, Clayton Pierce. Close yer eyes and hum a tune yer mother sang to ye. She'll join her voice with yers, right here." Maggie drew his hand onto his chest. "She'll always be right here with ye."

He nodded, his shoulders slumping as he accepted the fact his mother was gone. When Maggie touched his shoulder, he laid his head in her lap and sobbed for his loss. She rocked him, made soothing sounds, and rubbed his back while he cried. As the afternoon grew late and the room darkened, he lifted his head.

"I was s'posed to take care of her. I was the man of our family, and she counted on me." His chin trembled again. "I failed, and now she's gone. I should have... should have—"

"'Tis not your fault, Clayton. The Lord had another purpose for her." Maggie smoothed back one of his wild curls from his forehead, then cupped his cheek. "It won't help to question why."

"But what will I do now? It was just the two of us, me and her. What will happen to me?" he asked. His red cheeks glistened in the fading light, still wet from his tears.

"That's da easiest part, don't ye know?" she answered, assuming he was imagining the workhouse. She couldn't allow it. His mother had been a good, hardworking woman. Paddy would understand. "Ye'll be comin' home with me."

"What will Mr. O'Brien say?" the boy asked, looking doubtful.

"What he always says. 'Welcome, boyo.' And then he'll give ye a long lecture about loyalty and earning yer keep." She stood and pulled the boy to his feet. "Now get yer clothes together. It's time to meet yer new family."

CHAPTER 1

Late September 1820
Gracechurch Street
Cheapside, London

Clayton Pierce drummed his fingers on the small walnut table next to the wingback chair, waiting for Paddy's answer. The Earl of Winston cleared his throat and sent a pleading look to the Irishman, who sat scratching his jaw, the light red stubble making a *scritch* sound in the silence. At the same time, Paddy's other hand stroked the wiry fur of Aonarach, his gray and white Irish wolfhound. A tea tray lay neglected on a side table of the parlor, the pot now cold.

He's thinking about it. Clayton shook his head. They had enough to contend with right now without adding a missing person, or missing persons, to the docket.

Lady Winston, sitting next to her husband on the chaise longue, smoothed her silk skirts and gave the dog a wary look before her kind brown eyes searched the Irishman's ruddy face. "Mr. O'Brien, we realize this is unconventional. Our… type usually try to make by-blows disappear, not search them out. I've only just learned of her existence, and as a mother, I implore you to help us."

"Why now?" Clayton narrowed his eyes as he watched the man's expression.

Winston ran a shaky hand through his black hair, the fine streaks of silver showing through his fingers. His dark eyes held Clayton's steady gaze. "The children are married, so the news could no longer discourage a good match. I must know what the girl's circumstances are. If they are in need of anything, I will provide it even if the gir—my daughter prefers no contact."

"Have ye tried to find Miss Horton before?" Paddy scratched his chin.

"Once, just after I found out about the babe. But the solicitor couldn't find a Marianne Horton in London, so we assumed she married and assumed a different name. Or that she'd died." He shrugged his shoulders. "I had a wife and children to think about. Digging any deeper could have led to… I realize this sounds callous, but I couldn't expose my heir and unmarried daughters to a scandal."

The countess fiddled with the satin ribbons of her bonnet, her light-brown hair neatly swept up beneath the straw rim. "My husband didn't want to hurt me. Ours did not begin as a love match. Our early years were difficult—"

"By the time my father died, I trusted her enough to confide my secret. Yet so much time had passed, and she'd just given me Alexander. And as I said, the first attempt to find Miss Horton had been unsuccessful. I took the coward's way out and kept silent."

"When he finally cleared his conscience," added Lady Winston, "I insisted we find out for certain."

"And now?" asked Paddy, one red brow raised over his curious blue eyes.

"I'd like to make amends, Mr. O'Brien."

Clayton gave an uncharitable snort. "Swoop in and rescue the poor illegitimate lass, play the hero for a day, and then desert her again. With a substantial purse to ease your guilt."

Paddy stayed Clayton's next words with a quick side-eye. *Blast! He's seriously thinking about it.*

"I need details, my lord." Paddy's voice had turned business-like, signaling to Clayton they would more than likely be taking the case.

Misinterpreting O'Brien's tone, the earl rushed to explain. "It's not what you might think. I was—" Winston gave his wife an apologetic look. "At eighteen, I thought I was in love with the steward's daughter. We became... involved."

Lady Winston stared at her lap while her husband entwined his fingers with hers. Their eyes met, and Clayton realized the couple did love one another.

"When my father found out, he was furious, of course."

"Of course," echoed Clayton sardonically.

The earl frowned. "He sent Miss Horton away while I was finishing university. I returned home to find her gone and myself betrothed." He gave his wife a small smile that looked more like a grimace. "Needless to say, I resented my wife at first."

"Did ye know da lass was with child?" At Paddy's question, Winston let out a long, ragged sigh.

"No. After I inherited the title and assumed full control of the estate and holdings, I found a letter in my father's desk from Miss Horton addressed to *her* father. She wrote to inform him that she'd had a healthy girl." His voice cracked, and he paused for a moment, staring blankly at the chains of puce roses on the wallpaper over Paddy's shoulder. "I don't even know the child's name."

He handed Paddy the letter.

DEAR PAPA,

I realize you may not care, but I feel obligated for my child's sake to write. I have given birth to a beautiful baby girl. May God be with you and forgive you, for I cannot.

MARIANNE

THE COUNTESS CONTINUED, "My husband found an entry in the estate ledger indicating my father-in-law had sent a substantial sum to Miss Horton after receiving the news. There were no other accounts after that. The solicitor was told to send the money to a London office."

"Our inquiry into the solicitor revealed he died about five years back and his office closed. Mr. Horton, our steward," the earl added, "had disowned her, so he could give us little information other than his daughter had been provided for. We didn't even have an address to begin our search."

"And what of this Marianne's mother?" asked Clayton, wondering how a woman could cast out her own child.

"Mrs. Horton died when Marianne was a child. There was an older sister, but she had left several years before I left for university." He fidgeted with the beaver hat on his lap. "Mari—Miss Horton was a good woman, so I assume she eventually married. Unless there is an unwilling husband involved, I believe she would want my daughter to at least know who I am, meet me, and decide for herself if she wants any contact."

"But if her parents refuse yer offer?" Paddy folded the

letter and handed it back to Lord Winston, his hand going to the wolfhound's head now resting in his lap.

"Keep it in case you need proof of who I am. If my olive branch is rejected, I will have you pass along my information, including the name and direction of my solicitor, in case the situation changes." The pleading expression had disappeared. The earl added in the tone of someone used to getting his way, "Please, I'll pay well to find my daughter."

"Why not go to a Bow Street Runner?" Clayton worried about the man's motives. He'd seen more than one peer lie smoothly.

"Confidentiality. No matter how honorable the Runners are as a whole, there are always loose lips. I've been told discretion is one of the benefits when hiring the Peelers. I understand you will need time to consider our case." He stood and replaced his hat, then jerked on his waistcoat, and turned to help his wife. "We will be at my townhouse in Mayfair. You have the direction."

"If we take da case," Paddy said as he rose to follow the couple to the door, "it would be at least a month before we could begin an investigation. There are other clients already on our docket."

"Understood," agreed Lord Winston. "I've waited over twenty-five years. A few months will make no difference."

"One other question." Paddy's blue eyes narrowed as he studied the earl and countess intently. "If ye've told Her Ladyship, why da secrecy?"

Lady Winston smiled. "While we would both welcome another daughter, she or her mother might not be so disposed. And if the young lady has no desire to meet us, we see no reason to bring the matter to the attention of our other children. It's really up to her."

"So, you're testing da waters?" asked Mrs. O'Brien as she bustled into the room with a fresh pot of tea. Her mostly auburn hair was knotted in a bun, the late afternoon sun catching bits of threaded silver.

The countess's smile was warm as she turned to the Irishwoman. "Yes, exactly."

"We hope to hear from you soon," the earl said as they took their leave.

Mrs. O'Brien *tsked* at the untouched pot on the side table, walked to the other end of the room, and poked at the burning embers in the hearth to stir the fire to life. "Well? What did I miss?"

The domestic came in and swept the deep-green Wilton carpet covering the gleaming oak floor of the parlor, dusted the frames and tinder box on the mantel, then picked up the tea tray. "Will you be needin' anything else, ma'am?"

"Aye, bring a decanter of whiskey, please." Mrs. O'Brien turned back to her husband. "I t'ink ye'll be needin' a wee nip?"

Paddy chuckled, pulled his wife into a hug, and gave her a loud kiss on the cheek. "How ye know me, Maggie luv."

"Ye old goat. Not in front of da boyo." She flapped her hand at him, hiding the stain on her cheeks. Then she swatted at the wolfhound as he tried to squeeze his big head between them. "Aonarach, ye jealous beast, not every show of affection is for you."

Paddy only laughed and kissed his wife's other cheek. "Now sit and we'll tell ye our tale."

Clayton observed the older couple with a smile. He'd watched the scene a hundred times since he'd come to live with them. No, since he'd joined the family. If he found a woman like Margaret O'Brien, his life would be complete. Not that he was in any hurry. It was a tall order to fill. He joined Paddy and Maggie, standing opposite the wingback leather chairs. Leaning against the mantel, he studied the miniatures of the O'Brien "clan" as they were called. All unfortunates plucked from the streets. All successful adults now, thanks to the love and guidance of this Irish couple. And all vital operatives of O'Brien's Investigative Services, nicknamed Paddy's Peelers by the Bow Street Runners they worked with.

"First, we'll check up on the good earl and make sure the chit isn't trying to blackmail him. He may want to find her in order to silence her." Clayton rubbed his jaw thoughtfully, realized what he was doing as he gave a smirking Paddy a side-glance, and shoved his hand in his pocket. "Any thoughts, Maggie?"

Mrs. O'Brien was appreciated for her uncanny ability to judge a person's character. Paddy never questioned her appraisal, much to Clayton's dismay, though he was forced to admit she'd never been wrong.

The plump woman raised a brow, her intelligent dark eyes catching the pocketed hand and smiling. "'Tis good to be thorough, I agree. But I t'ink Lord and Lady Winston are sincere."

"Why?" Clayton was always amazed at the crumb she would pick from a conversation when assessing someone. He considered himself an astute observer, but Maggie always found the one bit he missed.

"When asked about da reason for secrecy, Lady Winston mentioned—"

"Another daughter? That's it, isn't it? You think she'll truly accept the girl." Clayton chuckled, proud of himself.

"Partly."

His grin faded as he racked his brain. With a sigh, he shook his head. "I give up."

Maggie gave him a wink. "She said they saw no reason to bring da issue to da attention of their *other* children. The countess included da unknown daughter as one of them, regardless of whether da lass accepts *them*. The woman will not only welcome da lass, but she'll make her part of da family."

Oh, how she knew his weak spot. He might as well face the inevitable. "And the earl?"

"If he wasn't sincere, why would he bother to tell his wife at all? He could easily have taken care of da matter without her knowledge. He wants to do right by his child—legitimate or not."

Clayton nodded and looked to the plastered ceiling, his cheeks puffed as he let out a long breath.

"'Tis a gift, I tell ye." Paddy guffawed. "Just accept it and be glad she's on our side."

CHAPTER 2

Mid-October 1820
Clement's Lane, Eastcheap, London

*T*he bell over the door of Madame Chapelle's tinkled a welcome, but it was drowned out by the *clunk* of a stout woman's boots. "Miss Chape-e-elle?" She took in several breaths, her large bosom heaving, and leaned on a chair for support. A lone white feather trembled atop her hat. "Lud, but it's a circus out there. Why must so many people be out and about?"

Genie rushed from the back, smoothing her dark-blonde hair and brushing off her skirts. "Mrs. Crawley, how good to see you."

"I need to speak with you." She waved her hand, then patted her mostly gray curls. "But first I need to sit. A cup of tea, please?" Her round face was flushed, the lashes on her bright but small blue eyes fluttered, and sweat beaded her forehead. "Unseasonably warm today, and the main thoroughfare is jammed with conveyances. Thought I'd save time and walk your lane rather than wait in that stifling carriage."

Genie settled the banker's wife in a chair and dashed to the back for a glass of lemonade. "Here, ma'am. This should help."

Mrs. Crawley took a big gulp, smacked her lips, and settled into her chair. "You always know just what is needed, my dear."

"Thank you, ma'am." Genie bit back the giggle by chewing her bottom lip. "What brings you here today?"

"For the same reason, of course." She wiggled her fingers beside her hat, the feather almost taking flight. "I adore this hat, and I'd like a spencer to match it."

"I see." Genie walked around the woman, her eyes narrowing as she took in the French silk bonnet of lilac. A thin chain of violet embroidery looped around paste amethyst stones sparkled when Mrs. Crawley took in a deep breath. Deep violet ruching and lace edged the large brim, while tiny clusters of the same flower wrapped around the center where the crown began. Behind the short crown fluttered the white feather.

Genie tapped her finger to her mouth. "Are you in love with the white feather?"

The woman's eyes grew wide. "I do enjoy my feathers."

"I don't mean to eliminate the adornment, just change the size and color." She fiddled with it, spreading it out and then curling it. "I'm thinking one of black and one of lilac, curled forward rather than standing straight up."

"Ooh, how daring. For day?"

"If anyone can pull it off, it's you Mrs. Crawley." Genie tapped her toe now along with her finger, then strolled to the counter where a sketchpad and pencils were kept. Her fingers flew across the sheet. She stopped, peered over her shoulder, then turned back, and finished the image. "A lilac silk with black and violet beading to mimic the amethyst. Perhaps some embroidered violets along the collar..."

"Oh, my dear, it's brilliant. I do believe your talent has surpassed your mother's. It must be the French blood." Mrs. Crawley rose, beaming. "No budget. Do what you will. How long do you think it will take?"

"I have your measurements, and as long as the silk is in stock at the draper's, I would say the end of next week?"

"You are a gem, my girl. A true gem."

After the banker's wife made her departure, Aunt Lydia emerged from the back of the shop. "Sounded like a happy customer."

Genie laughed. "She's really not hard to please and has referred us often. I told her the spencer would be done next week."

Aunt Lydia shook her head, her mobcap perched cock-eyed on her fading light-brown frizz. "Have you noticed the piles in the workroom?"

"Yes, but she's a steady customer. I'll work on it in the evenings. Mrs. Crawley is a dear."

"You say the same thing about most of the women who waltz through the door."

It was true. Genie liked people in general, but she didn't consider herself naïve. A young woman growing up without a father, pretending to be half French, and managing a business could not afford to be gullible. Her mother had learned that lesson, passing it on to her daughter every day until her sudden death.

Her aunt, Lydia Peckton, was her only family and business partner. Genie loved her like a second mother, but she knew what always followed such a statement.

"If only you thought the same about the men you meet."

There it was. The push to find a husband when she was perfectly content with her life.

"Your mother would be—"

"Happy I learned from her mistake," finished Genie. "I won't put myself through the misery. Mama gave her heart to a man, had it shredded, and regretted it the rest of her days."

"She never regretted having you, luv." Aunt Lydia put an arm around Genie's shoulders and squeezed. "And Mr. Peckton was the best of men."

"You were lucky."

"And you could be too." Her aunt's brown eyes, so like her own, sparkled with bits of gold when she smiled. "All men are not rogues. There are still some good ones to be found."

"But I'm not looking, so the conversation is moot."

"George is sweet on you." Her aunt's thick eyebrows waggled. "Stars in his eyes every time he picks us up in the carriage."

"He's a lonely widower with a daughter almost as old as I am. Why won't you believe it's you he's interested in and not me?"

She waved away the statement, though red crept up her neck. "But he doesn't look his age. Broad shoulders, muscled arms, not a bad face."

Genie closed her eyes. "No, he has a very kind face. But he stutters every time he speaks to us."

"He'll get over his nervousness."

"It's been three years."

Aunt Lydia picked up the sketch Genie had done for Mrs. Crawley. "This is lovely. I heard your description. Would you like me to pick up the silk tomorrow when I pick up supplies?"

"Yes, Auntie, I would appreciate that." Finally, on to a new subject.

The bell tinkled again, and another older woman entered. Genie's smile was genuine.

"Mrs. O'Brien, how wonderful to see you again. How have you been?"

"Feeling as old as Methuselah after my birthday last month," the Irishwoman replied with a grin. "I need a new gown. Mr. O'Brien reminded *me* our wedding anniversary is coming up. He wants to take me out on da Town."

"He's a good man, Maggie," said Aunt Lydia. "I was just telling Genie how she should be putting herself out there for the gents to see."

Genie rolled her eyes. Not twice in one day. And now her aunt had reinforcement.

"She's right, lass," agreed Mrs. O'Brien. "My Paddy may not be a thoroughbred, but he's da sweetest and steadiest of da work ponies. He'll never let me down. I can't imagine life without da stubborn oaf."

"Instead of wasting your efforts on me, why don't you convince my aunt that Mr. Lockwood has eyes for her. Perhaps it's time for *her* to search out a husband."

"Oh, da man's made a cake of himself for years over Lydia. Calf-love since she was a young widow."

"I couldn't be disloyal to my dear departed husband. Peckton was the love of my life."

Throwing up her hands, Genie turned toward the work-room. "I'll leave the two of you to sort out the details—*of the dress*. Call for me when you're ready for a sketch."

Once she was settled by the window, St. Clement's Church just within her view down the street, her mind wandered while her fingers moved with practiced ease stitching a hem. Third generation modiste. Her grandmother had owned a shop in a small village in Northumberland. She had trained Genie's mother, who had trained Genie in turn. She would always wonder what that little shop looked like, the village where her mother had grown up.

Stop daydreaming, foolish girl.

She knew she wouldn't be welcome if she did get the nerve to visit. Her grandfather, according to her mother, had made it perfectly clear she and "her bastard" would never be accepted if they tried to return. Her mother had fled to London and searched out her older sister. Within six months, Genie had been born, and her aunt had become a widow.

The Lord giveth and he taketh away. Her mother's words came back to her now. Was it true? Was God like a merchant, a tit for a tat? It wouldn't surprise her after listening to some of the fiery sermons at the church.

Aunt Lydia had joined Mama, both taking care of her and working as seamstresses for rent. They had worked hard to open Madame Chapelle's, and Genie was determined to see the business thrive.

Finishing the hem, she set it aside and began measuring the material for a ball gown. Her aunt and Mrs. O'Brien's laughter floated into the workroom. The women had been friends since Aunt Lydia had moved to London as a young bride.

Brides and weddings. Suitors.

What would it be like to attend a ball? Waltzing with a handsome man, drinking champagne, being *courted*? In some ways, she envied the young ladies who strolled in Hyde Park, putting themselves on parade to attract a husband. Those ladies would never understand deadlines that had to be met, bills to be paid, customers to coddle.

On the other hand, she had more freedom, more choices than London's debutantes would ever have. She was in charge of her own future and could choose her own destiny, without the heavy shadow of pain she'd seen in her mother's eyes every day. Those wealthy young misses had to obey a father and then a husband. Genie could sell her shop and move. To France to meet her relatives, she thought with a snort.

"What are you laughing at?" asked Aunt Lydia. "We're ready for a sketch."

The two women had pulled out several fabrics and colors, and different accessories filled a basket. Fashion magazines were scattered about. "It seems you want more than just a gown." Genie fingered the rich Egyptian-brown satin. "This will look lovely with your hair, Mrs. O'Brien."

Within the hour, there were several sketches joining the basket of accessories. Aunt Lydia wrote a ticket for the sleeveless gown, spencer, and redingote, adding the beads, embroidery, lace, and ribbons. It would be costly, but the O'Briens could afford it. Her husband ran the very successful O'Brien's Investigative Services. It was said his men could track down anyone. Their reputation was well-known and utilized by the magistrates of Bow Street.

"Such a talent," exclaimed Mrs. O'Brien. "Now if ye could only draw me to look as lovely wearing dem!"

"Thank you." Genie still blushed when complimented, much to her dismay. Of course, she was adept at sketches. It was her job. Yet, the praise always filled her with warmth—and embarrassment. "And don't be a goose. You will look stunning in these."

"Gets the talent from her mother," added Aunt Lydia.

As Genie collected the materials in one arm and the basket in the other, she realized the room had gone oddly silent. She looked up to find both women staring at her. A slight smile turned up her aunt's lips, and Mrs. O'Brien's dark-chocolate eyes sparkled with mischief.

"What?" she asked, unease prickling her skin. "I don't like the expressions either of you are wearing."

"We were just thinking," began her aunt, "that it's been so long since you and I have been out for an evening."

Genie shook her head, praying this wasn't leading to—

"Won't ye come to dinner next week? We'll have a grand time with good food and company, some parlor games or music or both. My Paddy does like a wicked round of whist, and Nora enjoys singing for a new audience." Mrs. O'Brien and Aunt Lydia both stared at her, heads bobbing up and down.

"Will it be a small party?"

"Very intimate, I promise," replied the Irishwoman.

"You and your husband, Miss Nora, and us?" Her gaze flicked between them, not trusting the complacent smiles. Too complacent.

And that glint in Mrs. O'Brien's eye had Genie worried. It mirrored the mischief in Aunt Lydia's.

CHAPTER 3

The following week
Gracechurch Street

"What do you mean the number is off?" Clayton had the perfect evening planned after a week of dead-ends on a case. A dinner at the Stock Exchange Coffee House, followed by a few drinks and rousing conversation. Perhaps a little gambling afterwards, the last of his imported brandy before bed, and a good night's sleep.

"I mean, we will have five at da table. An odd number makes it awkward if we play any parlor games afterward. Nora will be here, and I hoped to have Sampson, but dat didn't work out."

"How convenient for him." With a sigh, he nodded and tugged on his cravat. Maggie knew her boys rarely told her *no*. "How long do I have to stay?"

"Ah, thank ye, Son. Just a couple o' hours past dinner if ye please."

"I don't think what pleases me has anything to do with this," he said, silently cursing Sampson, the respected Dr. Brooks.

"Lydia needs some cheering, so I invited her and her niece."

"Niece?" He *knew* she'd been scheming. "Who happens to be young, beautiful, and unmarried?"

"Aye, but 'tis only a coincidence. The lass has assured her aunt numerous times she has no desire to be courted. Everythin' is not about ye, Clayton." She reached up and patted his cheek. "Thank ye. Now be sure to wear something nice. First impressions, ye know…"

Everything is not about you. She'd certainly put him in his place—and with a smile and a pat on the cheek. *Blast!* How did the woman do it?

He donned his greatcoat and headed out. Gus was meeting him at the Dog's Bone, and he hoped to hear some good news. It was a chilly day, though the sun shone brightly. He walked swiftly along Gracechurch Street, then continued as it became Fifth Street. Carriages and men on horseback moved both ways along the wide avenue, becoming more congested as he reached Thames Street and turned right.

Near Bush Lane, he entered the Dog's Bone, hearing the rowdy laughter of male customers before he neared the door. The tavern was crowded as usual. To his left was a long oak counter with Max, the barkeep, behind it, yelling over two men having an argument. The bald man paused to nod at Clayton. To the right were tables and a substantial hearth, where a large cast-iron pot sat bubbling with the day's stew. And if he was lucky, Max's wife had fresh biscuits in the kitchen.

"Pierce!" called a familiar voice. In front of him, at a table with several other men, sat Gus. Clayton watched as he stood and waved. As if anyone could miss the bear of a man.

August Rutland was built like Paddy with a barrel chest and massive arms and fists, but his extra height—well over six feet—often frightened the pads and vagabonds without a word spoken. His longish dark hair was pulled back in the usual leather tie, and he wore only his waistcoat with the sleeves of his white linen shirt rolled up over his muscular forearms.

Not for the first time, Clayton thanked the stars the man was on their side. A barmaid jostled against his side, hands fisted with several bumpers of ale. "Pardon me, Mr. Pierce," she mumbled and hurried to a nearby booth. Gus nodded his head toward the back of the tavern, and Clayton followed. Both men had to duck under the doorjamb as they entered a back room that looked much like it had two hundred years ago. Shelves lined the stone walls, overhead low charred timbers from years of smoke forced Gus to duck whenever he entered, and their heels clicked on the flagstone. A fire in the hearth crackled cheerfully, and bread and cheese sat on a table along one wall.

This was Max's private office and storeroom. Behind them in an alcove was the best of his brandy and ale. It was also a place where the Peelers often met to discuss the progress of a case. Paddy had never felt the need to have an office since their work was done on the streets. Cases were mostly referred, and meetings with clients were usually arranged at their home or a neutral location. Paddy insisted the Peelers were constantly roaming the neighborhoods, keeping contacts and making new ones, maintaining trust between themselves and the locals who often provided much-needed information.

"What do we have so far?" asked Clayton as he poured ale from a waiting pitcher into his cup. He raised an eyebrow at Gus, who nodded, then poured a second bumper.

"The three men arrested yesterday for the counterfeit

coins insist they don't know who their employer is. A man with a full beard watches the door when they arrive, brings them food midday, and searches them before they leave." Gus's coffee-colored eyes narrowed, as if remembering something. "They were paid well for making the fake guineas and didn't ask any questions."

Clayton nodded. "I'd wager the beard is a disguise. They're only one small piece to the puzzle. My hunch is there are rented offices and shacks all over Whitechapel and the rookeries just like the one we found. The Home Office is more concerned with the banknotes."

"What we uncovered is only a screen to keep us from the real operation?" Gus grunted and took a pull from his ale. "Could be. Or using the coin to pay off the riffraff they employ and saving the banknotes for the real swindle."

"Paddy is sure *this* gang is connected to the banknotes found. I saw one—they are excellent imitations. I wouldn't know the difference if I hadn't been trained to spot the irregularities."

"Probably why there have only been a few found in England. However, an agent has discovered more abroad." Gus cut off a hunk of cheese and tore off the end of the loaf of bread. After taking a bite of each, he said with a mouthful, "I suppose our next step is to bring in Walters."

Sir Harry Walters was the oldest of the Peelers, and the first waif brought home by Paddy. He was the unofficial second-in-command and a master of disguise. Walters's specialty was infiltration, making himself a familiar part of any group, any background.

"Lady Matilda won't like it," Clayton said with a chuckle, wondering when Harry would finally marry the woman. After he'd been knighted for his help with the Cato Street Conspiracy, the Earl of Darby had approved Walter's courtship of his sister.

"She won't know. And he won't let anyone else do it." Gus took another gulp of the ale. "I'll keep tracking and closing down the coin makers. Maybe I'll turn up trumps and convince one of them to talk."

"More than several inmates of Newgate would swear to your powers of persuasion, Brother," Clayton agreed with a smile. "I'll let Paddy know what's happening when I see him tonight. In the meantime, you track down Walters."

"Maggie invited you for dinner?" To Clayton's amusement, the big bear sounded hurt.

"I think she's playing matchmaker, so don't put the lid on your steaming kettle. Unless of course—"

"No, thank you. One woman ripping my heart in pieces is enough torture for me." Gus tore off another hunk of bread and stuffed it into his mouth. "She'll come round, though."

Clayton shook his head. Gus Rutland was the victim of unrequited love when it came to fiery-haired Honora O'Brien, the only orphan to whom Paddy and Maggie had given their name. She'd been abandoned as a babe and raised in a household of "brothers." While five of the boys loved her like a sister, Gus's affection was of the romantic kind.

* * *

GENIE GLARED AT THE MIRROR, then silently cursed her aunt. She knew this was a matchmaking affair, but she'd been up against a middle-aged matronly force.

Choose your battles! she thought wryly.

Her aunt had coiled her thick waves into a loose chignon, wrapped with a deep-blue ribbon that matched her mazarine gown. Ringlets spilled from the knot to tickle her nape. Delicate yellow paste diamonds the same shade as her hair decorated the simple blue headband. A heart-shaped locket of her mother's hung just above the modestly cut neckline.

"Simple, yet elegant," said her aunt from the doorway.

"It's what we're known for, isn't it?" Genie reached for her reticule and joined her aunt on the landing. "Shall we?"

The carriage waited in front of the shop. Madame Chapelle's had an arrangement with the livery a block away. They provided and maintained the postillions' uniforms for the rented conveyances in exchange for transportation. It was very convenient for both women and provided male protection when they went out alone. Though Mr. Derby employed over a dozen drivers, it was George who almost invariably escorted them about Town.

"Good evening, Mr. Lockwood," Aunt Lydia said as the driver helped them into the carriage.

"Evenin', ma'am," he said with a smile, his hazel eyes avoiding their gaze.

The night was thick with the inevitable London fog, making the streets slick and shiny. The weak glow from the streetlamps did little to thwart would-be pickpockets and thieves. They pulled to a stop in front of the O'Brien house.

"We'll be a few hours, Mr. Lockwood," her aunt told him. "Please don't wait out here the entire time. Go get yourself an ale or warm spiced negus and come back around eleven?"

"Whatever you wish, ma'am." He bowed and tipped his hat.

"You're much too good to us, George," she said quietly as Genie turned toward the house, smiling at the longstanding game they both played.

"Nay, ma'am, it's always my pleasure."

It was a three-story brick building with a wrought-iron fence and an inviting walkway and steps. The large door had been painted a vivid green in typical Irish tradition, and the large brass knocker was shaped in the image of a Celtic griffin.

Genie picked up the winged lion and rapped on the door.

It was answered by the maid, who collected their redingotes, hats, and gloves. *Let's get this over with,* she thought with a grimace.

"At least try to have a nice time this evening," Aunt Lydia murmured in her ear as they were led upstairs to the parlor.

Had she said that out loud, or did her aunt know her so well? Either way, it brought a smile to her face as they entered the room. Mr. and Mrs. O'Brien were sitting on wingback chairs by the hearth, and Honora sat at a harp in the far corner, strumming a soft Celtic melody. Her deep-red tresses spilled over one shoulder, and the expression on her face told Genie she was lost in her own musical world.

"Ah, a good evening to ye, ladies," said Paddy as he rose and moved toward them. A great beast followed like a gray shadow. She realized it must be the Aonarach, the wolfhound. Paddy bowed over each guest's hand as his wife came up behind him.

"I'm so glad ye both made it," said Maggie as she hugged her old friend and patted Genie's cheek. "A glass of ratafia?"

"Yes, please," they both said at once, then laughed.

"I'll have one too," said Honora, maneuvering the harp back into position and rising from the stool. "It's good to see you Lydia, Genie." She nodded at each of them, then her green eyes flashed to the parlor door. Genie sat on the chaise longue and turned to follow Honora's gaze.

Her pulse increased as she took in the handsome gentleman who had entered. Thick auburn waves curled around his ears and collar. She could almost imagine the red streaks the summer sun would add. His eyes were the same color as Honora's but a darker tint, more of a mossy tone. The kind of eyes that would absorb the surrounding shades, like the London fog outside the window.

Mrs. O'Brien stood and waved him in. "There ye are,

Clayton. May I introduce Miss Chapelle? And of course, ye already know Mrs. Peckton. This is Mr. Pierce."

"Always a pleasure, ma'am," he said as he moved across the room and bowed over her aunt's fingers. He then extended his hand to Genie, and the touch sent a bolt of awareness up her arm. "Miss Chapelle."

He bent toward her, the fine material of his jacket stretching across broad shoulders. His eyes twinkled—with mischief or interest? She guessed both, and it brought a smile to her face, which in turn brought one to his. It deepened the lines in his cheeks.

Heavens, he is handsome!

"A drink, Clayton?" asked Honora, her gaze darting between her brother and Genie.

"No, thank you," he replied, continuing to stare at Genie. "I am to tell you that dinner is served."

"About time," grumbled Paddy, rubbing his stomach. "I'm wastin' away ta nothing."

Genie pulled her fingers from Mr. Pierce's firm grip, and almost giggled at his expression when he realized he still held them. His firm lips turned into a grin, revealing straight white teeth. Her stomach did a little flip.

"Forgive me," he murmured as the others rose. "I wasn't expecting someone so... lovely."

"Why, thank you. I admit I'm also pleasantly surprised." His timbre was deep and inviting. It held the warmth of a hearth fire. Not the hot flames that first reached for the chimney or the glowing embers near their end, but the comfortable, heated crackle which promised a welcoming and cheery evening.

Where had Mrs. O'Brien been hiding him?

CHAPTER 4

*C*layton observed the beauty who had been conveniently seated to his left. Thick waves the color of golden wheat twisted at the back of her head, with tendrils curling artlessly to brush against her nape. She had a long, graceful neck that begged for a man's lips. Her fingers were slender, and the pads showed a woman who worked. With gloves, she could easily be mistaken for a member of the *ton*.

Her dress and manner were above reproach, and her speech, while not as cultured as the upper class, held no hint of cockney. More northern England, perhaps. He'd seen a nervous caution in her amber eyes which dissipated by the time they'd finished the ham and leek soup. Had she been on her guard or only shy? Trouble in love or only with conversation?

"Would you care for some roasted mutton or fricassee of chicken?" he asked as he took a portion of the mutton for himself. "I'll tell you a secret—only Maggie makes the potato pudding. Paddy won't allow Cook to attempt one of his favorite dishes. Says a bad one would ruin his taste for it."

"Then I must have some of the pudding with the chicken." She smiled at him, a kind and gentle expression that drew him to her. "So, tell me, Mr. Pierce. What sort of work do you do? Are you involved in the family business?"

He chuckled at the term. "Yes, I'm an investigator, or a Peeler as we're called by the Runners."

She took a bite of chicken and closed her lids, an *mmm* escaping her throat. When she opened those nut-brown eyes and caught his stare, she realized she'd made the noise aloud, and her cheeks grew pink. "I beg your pardon. But I'll share a secret with you in return. Aunt Lydia has an aversion to moist chicken. She roasts ours until it's dead twice over."

Clayton laughed, enjoying the amusement turning up her plump lips. "Then I understand the passion for the dish."

"Tell me," she asked, taking another bite of chicken without a moan this time, "what type of education or apprenticeship prepares you for such a... position?"

"Life with the O'Briens," he said with a wink. "As you know, our family has been gathered over the years rather than birthed. Paddy would find our strengths, our talents, and hone them until they were skills we could use within the agency. Of course, we all had to spend time working under the Bow Street magistrate. It was the basis for our knowledge of crime and investigation."

"So, all of you are required to work for Mr. O'Brien?" Her pale brows scrunched together. "It doesn't sound so... benevolent when it's put in such a way."

"Egad, no. He wouldn't have any of us in the agency who didn't want to be there. It's more of an honor, you see. To be plucked from a bad situation and brought into the O'Brien clan is like a gift from Heaven. Saved me, to be sure." He took a sip of wine, searching for the words. "I'd give my life for those two. All of us would. But if I wanted to walk away, I'd go with their blessing, excellent references, and a set of life skills in my pocket."

"And in return?"

Twirling the glass stem between his fingers, Clayton considered what they had given back to the O'Briens. "We love them as we would our own parents. When a child comes through their door, the first promise is of loyalty—not only to them but to all under their roof. Family is of the utmost importance to them."

Miss Chapelle nodded when he lifted the decanter of wine, and he poured her another half glass. "Then?" she asked as she took a sip.

"They provided our basic needs, shelter, food, clothing, and affection. There were never any favorites, except for Nora."

The fiery redhead's green gaze narrowed on Clayton when she heard her name. "What about me?"

"The favorite," he said simply.

Honora grinned. "There should be some benefit when a poor girl is raised with six monstrous brothers."

Maggie *tsked*. "Showing your jealous streak again, Clayton?"

"Not at all, just giving Miss Chapelle a little background. My original statement was there *were* no favorites among us until—"

"Dat little bawling beauty was dropped on our doorstep," said Paddy. "My Maggie took one look at her and fell in love."

"Ye were da one who insisted we needed a babe in the house," Maggie reminded him.

"And it wasn't truly on *their* doorstep," added Nora. "I was left at the foundling hospital. When the nurse saw my red hair, she called Maggie, knowing she'd wanted a babe but had never been able."

"We've sent a bottle of fine Irish whiskey to her every year since." Paddy scowled. "Nineteen bottles I could have drunk myself."

"But I'm worth every drop," Nora quipped.

"Every drop, and then some," Paddy agreed with an affectionate smile. He cleared his throat, obviously uncomfortable with the emotional turn of the conversation.

"So, all the boys became investigators?" Miss Chapelle looked from the O'Briens to Clayton.

"Fortunately, our boys have a variety of interests. Sampson loved his books, reading about plants and medicine. He's now *Dr.* Brooks," Maggie said, the pride evident in her voice.

"He patches the men up if they get hurt during their investigations?"

"Aye, dat and other t'ings," Paddy said, knowing his wife would have a fit if he mentioned autopsies during dinner.

"Benjamin was fascinated with rules and da law. Our own little enforcer when he was a lad. He's now our solicitor and helps bring certain cases to court." Paddy grinned. "Our symbol is the griffin—good against evil, light over dark."

"Loyalty and strength," added Clayton. He glanced at Mrs. Peckton, who was watching her niece with a curious smile.

Maggie continued, "Our youngest, Eli, is working as a Bow Street Runner now. I'm not sure which path he will take. He finds da work interesting, but he's an artist at heart. The boy can create a life-like sketch from someone's description. Person, place, animal."

"Genie has a talent for drawing," spoke of Mrs. Peckton. "Anything I try looks like a child's scribbles."

The second course was brought in, and while they dined on boiled turkey with wine and butter sauce, braised beefsteaks, and a meat pie, the conversation grew livelier. His dinner partner had a knack for getting him to talk, always turning the subject back to him, so he'd learned little about Miss Chapelle's background. Laughter mingled *oohs* and *aahs* when a plate of candied fruits, cheeses, biscuits, and jellies was set before them.

Clayton enjoyed watching the expressions that crossed Miss Chapelle's lovely features. Perhaps, just perhaps, Maggie had been right. Of course, he'd never admit it to her out loud. He wondered what entertainment was planned for after dinner. He hoped Paddy would play the fiddle, for the thought of taking this delightful woman in his arms in a reel had become very appealing.

"Miss Chapelle, do you like to dance?" The words popped out of his mouth before he could stop them.

CHAPTER 5

*H*er stomach was in a knot. Dancing? This wasn't a ball. Genie was sure her grip on the wine glass would snap the stem. Her mother had taught her some country dances. During Christmastide, they would invite Mr. Derbin and the postillion drivers from the livery for wassail and music and dancing. But it was more swinging from arm to arm than organized steps.

"I, uh—"

"She loves to dance," said her aunt. "Country reels, mostly."

Genie closed her eyes. *Gah!*

"Paddy, would you play for us?" asked Mr. Pierce.

Honora stood up. "I'll play the fiddle, so Mama and Da can dance."

"I'd be happy to accompany you on the pianoforte," added Aunt Lydia, "leaving two couples for a cotillion. Then we can take turns."

Genie glanced sideways at Mr. Pierce. He was watching her, and his grin was infectious when he caught her look. "Fine, dancing it is."

In the parlor, Mr. O'Brien poured a whisky for himself and Mr. Pierce. The ladies had madeira, which Genie had never tasted before. It was a wicked liquor—sweet and warm going down the throat. She'd have to be careful.

The parlor was nicely decorated; the walls had rows of roses against a creamy background. The thick wool Winton carpet matched the tiny leaves on the wallpaper. She touched one of the wingback chairs and found the leather soft as butter. She seated herself on the chaise longue, covered in a rich burgundy brocade, now pushed back along with the chairs to allow room for the entertainment.

"Shall we?" asked Mr. Pierce just as she had taken another sip of the wine. He took the glass from her hand and set it on the ornately carved mantel. She rose and bit her lip as Aunt Lydia settled herself on the bench, rifling through the sheet music.

"Nora, dear," called her aunt, "how about this one?"

Honora crossed the room, fiddle under her arm, and peered over Aunt Lydia's shoulder. "Perfect!" she said, turning to the couples and placing the fiddle beneath her chin, bow hovering over the strings. "On four." She tapped her foot, and on the fourth beat, the pianoforte and violin blended together, and the tune began.

The first of the eight-beat melody allowed the dancers to bow and curtsy to one another. She could feel the heat of Mr. Pierce's shoulder next to her, though they didn't touch. Across from her was Mr. O'Brien, with Mrs. O'Brien across from Mr. Pierce. As she raised her leg and began the dance, her trembling fingers hidden in her skirts, her inner voice counted the steps.

One and two and three and four, she met Mr. O'Brien in the middle and raised her hand to touch his as they passed one another. *Five and six and seven and eight,* she took his place on the opposite side and turned. The easy part.

One and two and three and four, she returned to the middle and touched Mr. O'Brien's hand again, but this time they remained touching as they passed, and she turned toward Mr. Pierce. *Five and six and seven and eight,* Mr. Pierce met her and raised his hand to hers. Heat rushed through her body. It had to be the madeira. But those sea-green eyes held hers.

One and two and three and four, she leaned toward Mr. O'Brien, sucking much-needed air into her lungs. *Five and six and seven and eight,* and then she was leaning into Mr. Pierce. So close she could feel his breath against her cheek, the smell of the whisky sharp to her nose, a devastating smile on his lips. She leaned again toward Mr. O'Brien, and when she returned to Mr. Pierce, he took both her hands in his warm strong ones, and they turned together.

While Mr. Pierce and Mrs. O'Brien took their turn, she chewed on her bottom lip and tried not to look at her partner's backside. But it was so firm, so round. Her mouth went dry, and she wished this was not a small gathering, and Mr. Pierce would have been obligated to keep his jacket on.

And then he was back, and they were holding hands. His skin against hers felt so natural, as if their palms had been waiting to meet. *Heavens, I'm foxed from two sips of madeira!* He squeezed her fingers, and the trembling ceased. As they made their turn, she was no longer counting. The rest of the dance was a blur of steps, and turns, and palms against palms, and the most stomach-fluttering gazes she'd ever experienced. A whirlwind of emotion flooded her as the music ended. Mr. Pierce tucked her hand into the crook of his arm and led her back to the mantel. With more restraint than she knew she possessed, she sipped the rest of her madeira rather than gulping it in one swallow.

"I believe Miss Chapelle has had enough dancing for now." Genie heard his deep timbre and peeked at him through her lashes as he loomed above her.

"A song, then! Da, join me," Honora called. "I'll play and you sing."

"What's your pleasure, lass?" he asked.

"Wild Rover," said Mr. Pierce. "One of Maggie's favorites."

"Wild Rover it is," agreed Honora. She turned to Aunt Lydia, found the sheet music, and they waited for Mr. O'Brien to join them.

"We add our voices on the chorus," Maggie told Genie. "Simple lyrics, ye'll have them down in no time."

The wavering keys of the pianoforte joined the whine of the strings, and Mr. O'Brien opened his mouth. A deep baritone, rich and pure, floated through the room, the words making Genie smile.

I'VE BEEN a wild rover for many's the year
  And I've spent all me money on whiskey and beer
  But now I'm returning with gold in great store
  And I never will play the wild rover no more

"HERE COMES DA CHORUS," whispered Mrs. O'Brien. Her clear voice added to her husband's, along with Aunt Lydia's. Then Mr. Pierce was beside her, whispering the words before they were sung, so she could join in.

AND IT'S NO, nay, never
  No, nay never no more
  Will I play the wild rover
  No never no more

. . .

45

EACH TIME the group finished the words "no more" the dog added his howl to the chorus of voices. Genie chuckled at the furry family member.

Mr. O'Brien continued alone with the humorous lyrics.

I WENT to an alehouse I used to frequent
 I told the landlady my money was spent
 I ask her for credit, she answered my nay
 Such a custom as yours I can have any day

THIS TIME, Genie was ready, and she belted out the words along with the others:

AND IT'S NO, nay, never
 No, nay never no more
 Will I play the wild rover
 No never no more

I BROUGHT from me pocket ten sovereigns bright
 And the landlady's eyes opened wide with delight
 She said: "I have whiskeys and wines of the best
 And the words that you told me were only in jest"

WHEN THE CHORUS BEGAN AGAIN, Mr. Pierce grabbed her hand and pulled her to her feet. His hand went around her waist, pulling her close, and he twirled in her a one-two-three rhythm as the song continued. She was breathless, laughing, and... happy! Happy as the heat of his body seeped into hers. Happy as he guided her across the room, light on his feet and, by turn, making her own steps light. Happy as he smiled down at her, reflecting her own exhilaration.

The tune ended, much to her disappointment. Her waist was cold where his hand had been, and a strange emptiness filled her as he returned her to the chaise longue and gave that charming smile to Mrs. O'Brien and her aunt. Genie sucked in a breath, tried to calm her pounding heart, placing her palm against her chest to smother the sound of the offending organ.

Then he was beside her again, hard muscle brushing against her side, his scent of bergamot and something masculine enveloping her senses. The warmth returned, and the hollowness vanished as he handed her another glass of madeira.

"Lud, but I haven't enjoyed myself so much in an age," exclaimed Aunt Lydia after another ballad. "I'd forgotten how beautiful your voice is, Paddy."

"I t'ank ye, ma'am. 'Tis been awhile since ye graced our abode." He gave the ladies a formal bow as they applauded. "May I include my talented musicians who made me shine?"

He held out an arm, and Honora stepped to his side and took a bow also to more applause, followed with a quick curtsy by her aunt.

To Genie's surprise, the evening ended much too soon. The O'Briens waved goodbye from the front door while Mr. Pierce helped the ladies into the carriage. Poor George had been waiting over an hour, but he smiled and clambered down to help Aunt Lydia. "You had a good time, then?" he asked.

"Wonderful," agreed Genie as Mr. Pierce assisted her up the coach step.

"Monstrous good," added Aunt Lydia.

Before Mr. Pierce closed the door, he took Genie's gloved hand and brushed his lips over the top. Heat pooled in her belly as he held her gaze with those mesmerizing green orbs. "It was truly a pleasure to meet you, Miss Chapelle. May I call upon you one day soon? Tea or perhaps a stroll through St. James's Park?"

"Yes to both!" cried Aunt Lydia.

Genie cast her aunt a horrified look, but Mr. Pierce chuckled. "Miss Chapelle?"

She nodded. "It seems my aunt knows me well."

As the carriage pulled away, she peeked out the window and saw him standing in the same spot, watching as they disappeared into the fog.

CHAPTER 6

"Should I send a note today or wait?" Clayton asked Maggie and Nora. "I don't want to appear anxious." He paced the room, his eggs and rasher now cold. Clayton had arrived at the ungodly hour of eight, a golden-haired beauty on his mind.

"Clay, dear, I've known ye since yer boots cost fourpence," Maggie said with a shake of her head. "I've never seen ye lack confidence with a woman."

"I think this may be a special lady, Mama." Nora sipped her chocolate, watching her brother. "The bow may have struck last night."

"Bow? What bow?" He ran a hand through his hair, wondering at his own agitation.

"Cupid's bow, you blunderbuss."

He sat down at the long table and looked at his cold meal, then took a sip of coffee and spit it out. Without a word, Nora rose and fixed him another plate and a fresh cup.

"So, what are you thinking?" she asked.

"Tea? A stroll through St. James's Park?" He let out a long

sigh. "Any suggestions? I'm used to being the one invited, then going along with whatever the lady prefers."

Maggie cleared her throat, and Clayton sent her a pleading look. "Genie works too much. If she spends too much time on pleasure, she'll feel guilty. What if ye combined da two?"

Clayton frowned. "How would I do that?"

"I know she orders material from certain drapers. In fact, Lydia happened to mention—"

"Just happened, mind you," interrupted Nora with a grin.

"Genie is going tomorrow. Mr. Derbin, the owner of the livery, usually sends round a coach, and da driver escorts her and carries whatever purchases aren't delivered."

"I should take her *shopping*?" A novel idea. "Would she like that?"

"Brilliant, Mama. Genie will be in her own realm, so to speak, and more comfortable. You can see how she interacts with others, observe her without being obvious." Nora waggled her red brows. "Look your fill, *boyo*."

With a frown at his sister, he stabbed his fork into the eggs. *Shopping*. It was better than an uncomfortable tea, the awkward silence as they searched for conversation.

"Of course, ye should offer to buy her tea and something to eat afterwards. Unless ye change yer mind in the meantime." Maggie brushed the crumbs of toast off her lap. "And if *she* has had a change of heart, then a polite *no* to yer invitation will let ye down gently."

Blast! The woman always had an answer. It was irksome, but he had to admit it was a fine idea. "Well, I'll send a note over right away," he replied, a knot of excitement in his belly. "I'll let you know how it all turns out."

"Exciting," said Maggie.

"To success," cheered Nora, raising her cup of chocolate.

* * *

"A NOTE FROM THE O'BRIENS' driver just arrived. He's awaiting a reply." Aunt Lydia waved the envelope above her head.

"And how do you know it's from a *he*?" Really, her aunt was almost annoying, she thought, snatching the note from the older woman. She chewed her bottom lip as she carefully broke the seal.

DEAR MISS CHAPELLE,

A little birdie told me you may have errands to run tomorrow afternoon. May I accompany you, and afterwards, perhaps I can take you for tea and a sweetmeat? I will have the driver await your reply for my time of arrival—if you consent to my invitation.

SINCERELY,
   Mr. Pierce

WINGS TOOK flight in her stomach, a smile forming unbidden to her lips.

"I knew it!" exclaimed Aunt Lydia. "Let me see."

She handed the paper over, already forming an answer. What harm would it do? If she was honest with herself, she *did* want to see him again. The thought of avoiding an awkward hour of tea in their small parlor, searching for conversation after the weather had been exhausted, was tempting.

"Well?"

Genie grinned. "I'll accept."

"That's my girl!"

* * *

IT TOOK an hour to decide what to wear. She finally chose a pale-green wool walking dress with yellow roses embroidered along the modest square neckline, cuffs, and hem. A yellow satin ribbon accentuated the high waist. Genie pinned the hat of the same color, with a circlet of dainty flowers brightening the crown, over her bun. Several long strands dangled along her cheeks, tickling her neck. She tossed the dove-gray redingote over her arm and descended the stairs to the shop.

"Aren't you looking lovely this morning," said Aunt Lydia over a mouthful of pins. "Mrs. Crawley made an appointment for her Queenie. She wants a matching coat for the spaniel."

"Another one? You'd think the dog was her child." Genie pulled back the lace curtain and peered out the window.

"It is her child since her daughter married and left for India. Now, *there* was a fine wedding. Her husband looked so handsome in his uniform." Her aunt pulled the pins from her mouth. "Are you looking for your beau?"

"He's not my beau."

"You danced, made eyes at each other, and he's calling on you. Definition of a beau if you ask me. Look it up in *Johnson's Dictionary*." She returned the pins to her mouth and poked one into the muslin fabric lying on the table. "I'll have this pinned and basted by day's end. You'll get the lace today for the trim?"

"Of course," Genie said, half listening. Would he be early, punctual, or late? She had no idea what kind of time manager the man was. She turned to look at the clock. At least another half an hour. She might as well start cutting the pattern for the next dress.

"He's coming at one, you say?" Aunt Lydia frowned when

Genie laid her redingote over a chair and removed a linen apron from a hook. "What are you doing?"

"Working, of course." Genie began to hum as she measured and drew off the pieces from the mock dress to form the pattern. "No one will ever accuse us of idle hands." She pictured her aunt's eyes rolling upward at the comment.

"Have I told you Clayton, er Mr. Pierce's story?"

Genie's hands paused. "No, I only know of Honora's." Was it a terribly sad story? Perhaps she didn't want to hear it quite yet.

"Maggie was friends with his mother. She came down with a fever. A few days later, Maggie went to check on her and bring some things. There was her poor little boy, not even ten yet, refusing to leave her body. Insisting his ma would wake up." Aunt Lydia shook her head. "The woman is a saint, I tell you. I was never blessed with a babe before my husband died, but I never went collecting children off the street. They could have been robbed blind or worse."

"And he stayed with the O'Briens after that?" What an oddly perfect solution the couple had come up with. Giving a homeless child a future and fulfilling one's maternal needs at the same time. "It takes a special kind of person to pull together such a family."

"Aye, she and her husband have the biggest hearts in London if you ask me."

The bell over the door tinkled, and both women looked at each other. One with wide eyes, the other's shining with mischief.

"Don't rush out, now. I'll tell him you'll be down in a few moments."

"You'll do no such thing. He'll believe me to be one of those vain, primping women."

They both rushed to the curtained doorway—it was a tie,

to be sure—and two bodies squished through, pushing up the drape.

"Ladies, please, there's no need to fight over me. Plenty to go around." Mr. Pierce removed his beaver hat and bowed, a devilish twinkle in his green eyes. One reddish-brown curl fell onto his forehead, but he swept it back under his hat as he straightened.

Genie brushed the end of the curtain off her shoulders, her hands going to her hair and hat out of habit. She sent her aunt a quick glare, which did nothing to wipe the ridiculous smile off Aunt Lydia's face.

"You're a punctual man," Genie noted as she looked at the clock ticking on the narrow mantel.

"I'm never late for important engagements." Oh, he looked fine. His shoulders filled every inch of his deep gray coat, and lighter gray trousers molded his muscled thighs. A burgundy- and gray-striped waistcoat added just the right amount of accent color.

Genie took a deep breath and let it out slowly. It was only a shopping expedition. Nothing out of the ordinary. Except for the swoonworthy man accompanying her.

How will I ever concentrate on length and price or add sums in my head with such a specimen beside me?

With a quick peck on her aunt's cheek, Genie retrieved her redingote and accepted Mr. Pierce's arm.

"It's a beautiful day, so I brought the curricle. We may not have many more mild days. One never knows about the weather in England except that it will always rain again. I've brought along a tiger, so we will have a chaperone and not cause any tongues to wag." He paused and looked down at her. The pulse in her neck sped up as his approving gaze took in all of her. "I apologize for rambling. Perhaps I'm a tiny bit nervous."

Genie let out the breath she didn't realize she'd been

holding. And when she took in air, the scent of bergamot and leather filled her nostrils. She decided it was one of her favorite scents. "To be honest, I am too. It's nice to know I'm not alone."

"How you could ever be alone is beyond my comprehension." Then before she could remark, he opened the door, placed a hand at the small of her back, and they passed beneath the chiming bell.

CHAPTER 7

*C*layton clucked to the pair of gleaming chestnuts, and the O'Briens' black-lacquered curricle eased into the traffic. Several passersby gave them smiling glances. They must look like a dashing couple. His chest swelled. *Don't be a peacock!* He gave her profile a side-glance. High cheekbones, straight nose, dainty chin below full lush lips— even her ears were the perfect shape and size. He cursed the usual confidence that had fled again this morning. *Traitor.*

The tiger was their boy of all work, Roger Lynch, with black curly hair stuffed under his hat and dancing green eyes. The strapping sixteen-year-old enjoyed wearing the uniform and standing on the back of the curricle about as much as he liked a proper bath. He preferred caring for the horses, driving, or running errands for Paddy. But the lad was determined to become a Peeler, and he willingly accepted any work the O'Briens gave him. Roger also had a deuced good right hook, which had aided Eli and Clayton in a tight situation on more than one occasion.

"Where to first, Miss Chapelle?" he asked as they came to the corner of Clement's Lane and Lombard Street.

"I can usually find the bulk of my items at Millard's East India House at 16 Cheapside." Miss Chapelle gave him a shy smile. "Whatever I can't find there, I should be able to purchase at Thomas & Co or Waithman & Sons on Fleet Street."

"Aye, aye, Captain," Clayton acknowledged with a salute as he guided the team to the left. He heard a satisfied grunt from his tiger at the mention of Fleet Street. With the notorious prison near those locations, he was glad to have Roger along.

He noticed Miss Chapelle's hands clasped tightly in her lap and wondered how to put her at ease. Perhaps the wares at the East India House would provide conversation she was comfortable with.

As he pulled up in front of the large building, Miss Chapelle's countenance brightened with enthusiasm. Ah, here she was in her element. "One of your favorite places, I gather?"

"Oh yes. Have you ever been inside?" she asked, her eyes straying back to the entrance. "The colors, the textures…"

Clayton nodded to the tiger. As Roger quickly jumped down and walked around to the front of the carriage to hold the horses, Clayton hurried to help Miss Chapelle down. He secured her gloved hand in the crook of his arm, remembering the feel of her skin when they'd danced at the O'Briens. A sizzle of desire danced through his belly. Why did she affect him this way? He knew females considered him to be a fine-looking man with a good income. It was easy enough to find a pretty companion for the theater or a dance. But none had caught his interest as the one now on his arm. It was as if… he'd been waiting for her. He shook his head.

You're no green boy. Get hold of yourself.

They entered a huge hall filled with dozens of customers.

Giant bolts of cloth, stored in hollow spaces near the ceiling, lined the two walls above the long counters where smartly dressed all-male clerks assisted the clientele. Long lengths were pulled from the bolts to drape across the walls so they could be pulled to an interested customer for inspection. There were muslins, satins, silks, tweeds, and linens of all colors imaginable, and various prints sported the flora and fauna of England and countries abroad. The noise level was high as people bickered about price or chatted with one another while they waited their turn.

"Oh my, it's busy. I'm afraid this may take close to an hour," she said in apology, her whiskey-colored gaze catching his.

"Not to worry. I have nothing else on my agenda this afternoon," he said with a wink, "except escorting a lovely lady around Town."

She laughed. "Well, I'm relieved. Follow me."

Miss Chapelle strolled the length of the store, passing some of the samples with barely a glance and stopping before others for several minutes. He could almost see her mind whirling with fashionable images as she chewed on a fingernail and tapped her toe. Then with a brilliant smile, she announced, "I've made my choices."

"Already? It hasn't been half an hour." This wasn't as painful as he'd imagined.

"Oh, no," she said with a chuckle. "Now we wait for assistance."

Clayton found the next thirty minutes to be a treasure of information about the lady. He watched who she nodded at, arched a brow at, or who received a smile or a curt nod. He asked her questions, which she readily answered. He learned her favorite color (blue like the sky), favorite food (cottage pie), and favorite sweet (lemon tarts). She did not like turnips, gossips, arrogant men, or gray days.

"And you?" she asked in return.

"Let's see. My favorite color is now amber because it's the color of your eyes, favorite food would be roast chicken, and my favorite sweet is custard with any type of fresh berries on top. I *do* like mashed turnips. I do not care for the on-dits unless I'm the one gossiping, goose—too greasy—or swine. Nothing personal against them, it's just the smell. Can't get past it." He took in a gulp of air as if he'd been speaking nonstop. "Did I cover everything?"

Miss Chapelle shook her head. "And more. Do you really like to gossip?"

He hung his head in mock shame. "I'm afraid I do, though only about my betters. Some of those lords and ladies are just a bit too high in the instep and deserve a good taunt."

"I agree, sir." She paused, her cheeks coloring. "Did your favorite color truly change because of the color of my eyes?"

A hand flew to his chest. "I would never mock *you*, dear lady. The truth is I didn't have a favorite color before."

A voice interrupted their conversation. "Miss Chapelle, how good to see again. What may I assist you with today?"

"Ah, Mr. Lecking, you're looking well." And with that, the shy miss vanished, and the owner of a busy modiste shop appeared.

She ordered the clerk to bring her this swath or sample, selected thread and ribbon, then waited for lengths to be cut. He rather liked this take-charge side of her. When her selections were gathered and checked, she signed the invoice and arranged for delivery.

"Very good, ma'am," said the clerk. "We hope to see you again next month."

The bright sunshine outside caused them both to squint while they searched for Clayton's curricle along the busy street. He spied Roger, his tall form standing in the vehicle and waving his arms. With a hand on Miss Chapelle's back, he guided her down the street. Once settled, he took the reins and clucked to the horses after Roger had resumed his position behind the seat.

"What adventure awaits?" he asked.

"I believe I'm quite content, sir," she answered. "And you?"

"Indeed," he replied, his eyes taking in her profile. "Except shopping seems to sharpen the appetite. May I tempt you with tea and a lemon tart, perhaps?"

"That would be lovely."

* * *

BY THE TIME Mr. Pierce brought her home, Genie's stomach was full and her mind in a jumble. She hadn't ever enjoyed a gentleman's company so much. Not that she had many—any—suitors. There had been a few before her mother's death, even a fairly regular caller. But when she'd become so busy with Madame Chapelle's, they had dropped off after too many refusals. By the time Genie turned twenty-six, she assumed she was on the shelf and had been content with her lot. She had dreams of traveling to Paris, a center of fashion, and perhaps one day, India. Oh, the colors would be stunning in an Indian market.

Before she'd removed her redingote, Aunt Lydia burst into the shop. "Well?"

Genie had wanted to put her off, tease her a bit, but she was spilling over with excitement. "I had a wonderful time."

"What did you do? Where did you go?"

"I ordered supplies from Millard's. It was quite busy, so we had a chance to talk while we waited our turn." She chewed her bottom lip. "He's very nice and put me at ease before we left the warehouse. Then he took me for tea and a lemon tart."

"Ooh, you love those. How'd he know?" Her aunt's brown eyes were wide. "I swear I didn't say a thing."

"No, we took turns sharing some of our favorites. He wants to call again." She removed her bonnet and walked toward the workroom. "I told him I didn't think we should. We would only encourage the matchmaking matrons."

A loud huff sounded behind her, and she grinned.

"You like him? Don't let two nosy women who care for you keep you from romance."

Genie turned to find her aunt with her hands on her ample hips, a frown on her face, and lips pursed. Then she saw the smile on her niece's face. "You're teasing. What did you really tell him?"

"He may call on Sunday for tea."

"Why, that's days away, Eugenia." The huff and scowl were back.

"I haven't been courted in six years. I don't think a few days will make much difference." But Genie silently agreed. "We have clothes to sew and clients to satisfy. Pleasure will be reserved for Sunday when the work is done."

But she could still feel his warm breath on her neck and his lips on her cheek. She shivered. It was like being nineteen again with the world full of possibilities and sunshine. Had she been lying to herself about being happy with her future? Would this be the man to prove her wrong? A tiny voice echoed in her brain.

I hope so.

CHAPTER 8

*C*layton needed to get his mind off Miss Chapelle. He'd see her tomorrow, and today there were counterfeiters to track down. He was waiting in the back room of the Dog's Bone for Gus, who was late, and it made Clayton nervous. Gus was never late unless…

He took a long pull of ale. He'd wait another hour but finish his drink in the taproom. Maybe one of the patrons had seen him. No use sounding the alarm to Paddy without tangible information.

"Rutland?" The barkeep shook his head. "Ain't seen 'im since yesterday, maybe the day before." The burly man wiped the counter with a large rag. The joke around the tavern was that Max kept his place as shiny as his head. "Ask Bess. She hears more than I do."

"Thanks, Max," he said with a nod. "I will."

Bess was more help. "He was in yesterday," she said, swiping at the brown hair escaping her mobcap. "With some old man I've never seen in here before. The man did most the talkin', and Gus nodded his head a lot."

"Thank you." He turned to leave.

"He's not in any trouble, is he? Can I help?" Her brown doe eyes shone with concern.

"You just did."

The woman still held a flame for Gus, even though he'd explained he only had eyes for Nora. A pair of love-unrequited muttonheads in his opinion.

As Clayton was leaving the tavern, Roger almost knocked him over. "I have a message from Mr. Rutland."

Clayton swore softly. "Is he hurt?"

Roger shook his head. "He was whole when I left him."

"Follow me." He returned to the back room. "Now tell me everything you know."

"We were watching two rascals come out of the boarding house, where he thought another *room* had been set up. So, we followed 'em." Roger accepted the bumper of ale and took a long, loud swig. "But it became clear they were headed toward Regent Dock, maybe the warehouses in Limehouse. So, I'm to get ye and bring ye there." He took another long pull. "With weapons."

"I'm never without, boyo," Clayton said, rising. He patted his sides where his Rigby pepperbox pistol was tucked into his trousers. He'd ordered the pistol from a well-known maker in Ireland. It had five barrels and a double-action trigger that allowed him five shots without reloading. "Do you have something to protect yourself?" He checked the sheath in his boot for his dagger.

Roger grinned and patted the blade under his jacket and two smaller throwing blades in his boots. "Ready, Mr. Pierce!"

The young man was too enthusiastic. "You follow my lead, understand? No fatalities tonight."

He nodded and followed Clayton out of the Dog's Bone and onto Thames Street, turning toward the Limehouse district inhabited by all sorts of seafaring workers and a large

Chinese population. Once they came to Narrow Street, Roger took the lead. He stopped outside The Grapes tavern, speaking low in Clayton's ear. The rough, boisterous patrons, inside and spilling out into the street, covered his words from passersby.

"Mr. Rutland thought they were heading toward one of these warehouses along Narrow. I assume they'd use a door off the alley. He'll be along here if he was right." Roger pulled his collar up against the evening fog settling in, and Clayton did the same. "Should we split up?"

Clayton shook his head, worried for the lad's safety. Roger had been raised on the streets of Whitehall, tough and experienced beyond his years, but still, he was only sixteen. "We'll stay together. I can send you for help if needed."

They quietly made their way down the alley and stopped at the end, near a back entrance of a warehouse. Distant shouts and laughter echoed behind them. Checking just inside the door, Clayton shook his head and turned to the right. Following the lane behind The Grapes, he stopped at the next warehouse and then another. At the last building along the alley, they found Rutland hunched behind several barrels.

Crouching next to him, Rutland nodded his head toward the back entrance. "I haven't been waiting long. Fine work, Roger," Gus said with a nod to the boy. "If we can find out what they are doing inside, we can send Walters this way. He'll figure a way to join 'em. There was a man watching the door."

"Where'd he go?" whispered Roger.

Gus grinned and leaned back, revealing a still body lying next to him, hands and feet tied and mouth bound. "He'll be coming with us tonight. I'm in a persuasive mood. Lad, I need you to keep an eye on him. If he stirs, plant him a facer with your wicked right."

"Yessir!"

Clayton pulled back the hammer of his pistol, and the two silently entered the warehouse. The bottom floor was dark and silent. Voices floated down from the next level, then footsteps on the stairs. Clayton pointed to an alcove below the stairs where they could hide.

"Ready for some cheap whiskey and a willin' barmaid," said the first man. "This place is right eerie at night."

"Where's the guard?" asked the second as he followed his partner into the alley.

"Looks like he took off. Told ye no' to pay him till mornin', din't I?" The voices faded.

Clayton pointed his finger toward the ceiling, and they crept up the stairs. The next floor had more light, the windows filthy but not blacked out. Peeking over the landing, Clayton saw oak barrels stacked along a far wall and two men sitting in chairs with pistols on their laps.

"That's them," whispered Gus. "Think they're running liquor?"

Clayton shrugged. This wasn't what he'd expected. No counterfeiting going on here. But something was amiss and warranted ruffians for guards. Should they confront the men anyway or back off and report to Paddy?

The decision was taken from their hands when the door below burst open. "Be alert," cried a man below.

"Bloody hell, we've been found out." Gus's huge form rushed past, pistol drawn.

A hammer clicked below, and Clayton turned, aimed, and shot. The man crumpled onto the bottom step. In the alley, he could see two dark forms wrestling. Roger and the dead man's accomplice. Where was the guard?

A loud smack, and one man fell to the ground. Roger jumped over the still body and took the stairs two at a time, right behind Clayton as he entered the second floor.

He and Roger rushed to join Gus, who stood with his pistol pointing back and forth between the two men, their weapons pointed back at their huge target. "Seems we have a stalemate."

"At least the odds are in our favor now," agreed Clayton. "Come now, gentlemen. I'm sure you have loved ones who you want to see again. Let's not do anything rash."

"It's you who won't be seein' anythin' after t'night," rasped a burly fellow. "I ain't goin' to Newgate fer nobody."

"Who said anything about Newgate?" Gus gave Roger a side-glance. "We just want to ask you a few questions."

"Ye jus' kilt one of our comrades. An eye fer an eye, I say." The taller, thin man with a crooked nose raised his pistol higher.

Clayton heard a soft *whoosh*, then Crooked Nose yelled, dropped his pistol, and grabbed at a knife in his thigh. The pistol discharged, Gus yelled out a curse, and Roger flew at the injured man. Behind them, two shadowy figures rushed the stairs. A fist smashed into Clayton's stomach, followed by another to his head. Knocked to the ground, he grabbed his assailant by the leg and yanked him off-balance. Another shot sounded behind him. A grunt, another bellow of pain.

Getting to his knees, Clayton scrambled for his pistol, aimed, and fired at the figure struggling to get up. The body lurched and then fell with a *thump*. Clayton turned and saw Roger, who had been circling Crooked Nose, another blade glinting in the lad's fist, fly into the stacked barrels as a fourth footpad crashed into the lad headfirst.

Clayton pointed his pistol at Crooked Nose. "Don't give me a reason."

A blur in his peripheral vision, a loud *crack*, and Roger was leaning over his unconscious attacker, rubbing his right fist against his thigh. His left arm sagged at an odd angle.

Rutland was on his knees, breathing hard. He fired at the burly man just as another shot rang out, then collapsed.

"Rutland!" cried Clayton, backing up to check on Gus and still holding Crooked Nose at gunpoint.

Roger ran across the wood planks and slid on his knees to a stop before the hulking form. "He's been shot."

When Clayton turned his head, Crooked Nose took the opportunity to make his escape. They could hear the ruffian fall over the dead body at the bottom of the stairs as Clayton rushed to help Gus. The burly man tried the same, and Roger went after him.

"Let him go," yelled Clayton. "We need to get Rutland out of here."

Gus groaned and tried to rise.

"Where are you hit?"

"A long way from the heart, ye nodcock. But bloody hell, it hurts." With another groan, Gus got to his knees. "Roger, are you hurt?"

"Not as bad as you, Mr. Rutland," he answered with a lopsided grin that turned to a grimace when he tried to move his left arm. "I think my shoulder's cockeyed."

Peering around the warehouse, Clayton counted one dead and one possibly unconscious man. Another body below. "How did the guard get loose?"

"Guess I didn't hit his friend hard enough. When he came to, he must have cut the ropes." Roger nodded at the other prone figure on the floor. "I'd say I did better with this one, eh?"

"I'll check those barrels to see what's hiding inside. Then we'll get you home."

As he moved, he stepped in something slick and almost lost his footing.

Blood.

Seeping from Gus.

"He got hit at least twice, Mr. Pierce," said Roger, eyeing the growing puddle with alarm. "It looks bad."

"God's teeth," mumbled Clayton. "Where?"

"Left arm, and my right side," groaned Gus.

The barrels would have to wait. A belly wound could be fatal. "Can you help me get him up?" he asked the boy.

Roger nodded. "My right side's good, so I'll take his left."

It took a quarter of an hour to make their way back to Narrow Street. Pretending Rutland was drunk and being helped home, the trio shuffled along until they reached Thames Street. Clayton hailed a cab, and they managed to get Rutland inside the hackney.

As soon as they reached Gracechurch Street, Roger jumped from the hackney and pounded on the O'Briens' front door. Paddy himself answered, but before Roger could speak, Clayton yelled, "We drank our last coin, Da. Can ye pay for the hackney?"

CHAPTER 9

"Maggie, some coin for the hackney if ye please," bellowed the Irishman. "The boyos are foxed again." He lumbered down the steps and caught Rutland's limp form to his chest as Clayton hoisted him forward. Then Clayton jumped down and took one side of the injured mountain, and he and Paddy hauled the body up the few steps, then sideways through the door.

"I gave him extra and t'anked him for keeping quiet," said Maggie behind them as she slammed the oak door shut. "What da devil happened?"

Clayton appreciated her no-nonsense tone after spying Roger's white face. The pain was catching up to the boy. "We'll take care of you," he said, lowering the lad into a chair. "You were a Peeler tonight, to be sure."

Roger smiled feebly and leaned back, his eyes closed, a hand clutching his shoulder.

Nora was in the kitchen and cleared the table for Gus. "How bad is it?" she asked, spying the blood on her da's shirt front.

"He took a shot to the arm and one on the side of his

belly. Maybe more." Clayton grimaced as he sat. *Deuced ribs.* His head was pounding, his jaw hurt like the devil, and his eye was beginning to swell. Nothing that wouldn't mend. "The bull still managed to walk between us until we made it out of Limehouse and found a hackney."

"You big galoot," mumbled Nora as she pulled open the bloody wool jacket and gasped. "Don't you dare die on me, Gus Rutland. Not tonight!" They heard the panic in her voice, and Maggie stepped in.

"Nora, go fetch Sampson, tell him to bring plenty of laudanum with him, and I'll start cleaning him up," ordered Maggie. "Paddy, get water on to boil. A big pot."

* * *

I⊤ WAS after midnight before Clayton breathed easy. Sampson stood over him with a decanter of whiskey. The physician's brown hair was tousled, and blood splattered his linen shirt and rolled-up sleeves. "Another? I think I will."

Clayton nodded. "Fine job tonight, Dr. Brooks."

"I'd like to respond it was my pleasure, but it wasn't. The bullet in his side might have killed another man. It still may if infection sets in," Sampson replied with a scowl, baring a dimple in one cheek. "But no one died on my watch, so all's well that ends well, eh?"

He lifted his glass, and Clayton, the O'Briens, and Roger did the same. Clayton gritted his teeth as pain shot through his bound ribs. He knew from experience it would take several weeks to heal.

They were in the parlor now, and Paddy had been informed of the evening's events. Nora sat with Gus in a servant's room. Sampson hadn't wanted Gus to attempt the stairs in his condition.

"How's the shoulder?" Clayton asked Roger. Sampson

had managed to put the dislocated joint back in place after the lad had thrown back a healthy dram—or two—of whiskey.

"Never better, Mr. Pierce," he slurred. "Never had better liquor, either."

"I think we've come to a point where you can omit the *mister*. I'm not sure we'd be alive tonight if you hadn't been with us."

"Well, then." The boy beamed. "Ye can call me Lynch. That's me surname. Got it from my da afore he ran off." Then his head drooped, and a soft snore filled the silence.

"What do ye t'ink they were paid to guard those barrels?" asked Paddy as he sipped his whiskey and stared into the fire. "Must be worth a pot o' gold to keep someone on watch all shifts. Gets a wee expensive, eh?"

"I assume it was alcohol of some kind. Avoiding the tariff?"

"T'ink about it again, boyo. What have I taught ye?"

"Never assume the obvious." Clayton drummed his fingers on the arm of the chair. "Powder of some sort? Gunpowder, perhaps?"

"More likely than rum or brandy. And how does it tie in with da counterfeit banknotes?" Paddy scratched his chin. "I'm beginning to t'ink the counterfeitin' is only part of a bigger scheme, not the main production."

"I'll return in the morning and see what I can find."

"Why wait till tomorrow what ye can do now?" Paddy stood and stretched with a loud yawn, calling Aonarach to his side. "We'll be back shortly, love. Sampson, would ye care to join us?"

"If you have an extra pistol. I was wearing my physician's hat when I arrived. It's been awhile since I've played investigator." He threw back the rest of his drink and turned to Clayton, his hazel eyes twinkling. "We can take my carriage to the outskirts of Cheapside, then get a hackney through Limehouse."

But the warehouse was empty. Two chairs where the guards had set and several bloodstains on the floor planks were the only evidence left proving *something* had been there.

"By the devil, if they aren't quick as slithering snakes," mumbled Paddy as they walked the length of the warehouse. "We hear the bees humming, but we see no honey."

Clayton let out a mirthless chuckle. "Indeed. Every time we get close, something goes awry. I believe you're on to something with the barrels."

Aonarach sniffed at the stained floor board, then moved toward the area where the barrels had been stored. He let out a howl. Along the wall, where the contraband had been stored, there was a small gray pile. Clayton dipped his finger in it, smelled it, then touched the tip of his tongue to the dust. "Gunpowder."

"But why would they need counterfeit banknotes to sell gunpowder?" wondered Sampson aloud. "Paying for it with the fake blunt and selling it for more to another buyer?"

Paddy shook his head. "They'd have been caught by now. If not by Bow Street or da Home Office, then by one of their swindlers when da cheat was discovered. This has been going on for months."

"The mystery deepens," mused Clayton. "This reeks of The Vicar." The nickname belonged to a demon that the Peelers had been tracking for two years. They would shut down one operation, only to find he had a dozen others still running. The villain had his fingers in every kind of illegal pot.

"Aye, and just like him to slip through our fingers again. But with each venture we eliminate, we take away one of his trusted inner circle." Paddy *tsked*. "Make da noose wide enough, and he'll eventually stick his neck in it."

* * *

"Now I KNOW why you do the baking," Genie said with a laugh, blowing a curl out of one eye. She had rushed through a few minor jobs earlier in the morning to have the afternoon free, and now she was whisking the eggs and cream for a custard. She didn't have fresh berries, but Aunt Lydia had produced a jar of strawberry preserves.

"Let me finish so you can change. Why not wear the green muslin with the light-rose embroidery? It makes your eyes shine, and you look so… feminine in it."

"You think so?" she asked, conjuring the image of the dress to her mind. "Do I want to appear so *feminine?* I would hate to give him the wrong impression. We are independent businesswomen, Aunt."

"But that doesn't mean a layer of femininity does not exist beneath our tough exterior," Aunt Lydia said with a laugh. "And be sure to pull those curls down to cradle your face."

"Yes, ma'am," Genie replied obediently.

An hour later, she peeked through the curtain to see Mr. Pierce arrive on horseback. A boy ran up to him, there was an exchange, and then the boy stayed with the horse while the man entered the shop.

She scurried down the third flight of stairs, reaching their second floor, careful to lift her skirts so she didn't trip. Genie wore sturdy half boots more than delicate satin slippers, and she would be sorely embarrassed if she took a stumble on the old wooden steps. But halfway down the next flight, she was surprised to meet him on his way up.

"Your aunt said she would join us shortly," he said as he

removed his beaver hat, the dark staircase casting his features in shadow. "She thought we would be more comfortable in your parlor than the workshop."

"Of course." She turned to retrace her path. *Lud, now he has a view of my backside.* Her face heated as she reached the entryway. "This way."

The parlor was her favorite spot in the house. Small and cozy, it had soft gray walls with a gray and burgundy floral-patterned couch facing the hearth. It was flanked by two rocking chairs with small twin side tables. There was a delicate silver filigree mirror above the mantel, where several framed miniatures displayed images of her mother, Aunt Lydia's husband, and Genie's grandmother. A handmade lace cloth covered the small dining table in the center of the room. It was a place of shared hopes and dreams, of women daring to be more than expected, of family. This was the space where all important discussions were held, and all happy announcements were revealed.

She turned and gasped. "Your face! Heavens, what happened?" He had a swollen blue and purple eye, a bruise on one cheek, and a scrape along his jaw.

"I tried to intervene in a heated discussion and got caught in the middle, I fear." He studied his polished boots. "An apology, Miss Chapelle, for my rough appearance."

"Oh dear." Her hand went to his cheek without thinking and delicately inspected the mark. "Does it hurt much?"

"I'm happy to say the other two are worse off," he said as his palm covered her hand and held it against his jaw. "But your magical touch just dissolved any pain I had."

They were standing close now, and she could feel his breath against the top of her head. If she raised her face, they would be close enough to…

She lifted her chin, and his mossy eyes stared into hers, a question hovering between them.

"May I?" he whispered, his tone husky.

Genie nodded, and his lips brushed hers, once then twice, before covering her mouth with his own. Her hands went to his chest, his hard chest. The pulse in her throat echoed down her body, and without thought, she grasped his waistcoat in her fists and lifted onto her toes. His arm went around her waist and pulled her against his body. So firm, so warm. She couldn't think. The world shrank to his lips on hers, his palm caressing her back, his scent of bergamot.

"I'm coming with the tea," called Aunt Lydia from the staircase. "Could you open the door for me?"

Genie jumped back, her hands smoothing her skirt, her eyes studying the gray wool carpet beneath her slippers. When she looked up, there was a smile in his eyes—eye, rather—and desire. "I've wanted to do that since we danced a week ago." His knuckles brushed her cheek as he stepped back and met Aunt Lydia at the door.

Her aunt was a wicked, conniving woman. She'd given them a bit of time alone. And now Genie was flustered and needed a fan. A very large fan.

"In a bit of a skirmish?" asked her aunt once they had settled before the fire, and Genie had poured for all three. They had both noticed his slight grimace when he'd lowered himself into the chair. "I assume you were the victor?"

Mr. Pierce laughed. "I'm afraid it wasn't of my choosing."

"I'm sure Dr. Brooks took fine care of you." Her aunt frowned and cast a glance at her niece, as if she knew something Genie didn't. "How is business?"

"A never-ending docket. There seems to be a multitude of people requiring investigations of some sort." He took a sip of tea, then reached for a biscuit.

"Don't fill up with too many biscuits. Genie made a custard, and it's cooling now." She stood and hurried from the room.

"You remembered?" His smile warmed her to her toes. "It wasn't necessary."

"Kind acts are never required, are they? Yet they are as beneficial for the one who gives as for the one who receives." She was mesmerized by his lips. Wanted to reach out and touch the bottom one. "As when you took me for tea and a lemon tart."

"I won't argue that afternoon was filled with pleasure." He paused. "I enjoy your company, Miss Chapelle. Would you do me the honor of seeing me on a more regular basis? Would you consider a courtship?"

CHAPTER 10

*T*he wings fluttered in her stomach, her head light. "I-I would... most definitely consider it," she stammered ungracefully. *Coward! Just say yes.*

Aunt Lydia saved her with the custard. They sat for an hour, discussing the weather, new businesses opening, others closing, and the past year with the newly crowned King George IV. Mr. Pierce was knowledgeable and had no objections to the ladies discussing politics. He was as refreshing as a May breeze.

Genie was disappointed when he rose to go. "May I walk you out?" she asked, rising and fetching his greatcoat.

"I'd hoped you would." There was a twinkle in his deep-green eyes that matched Aunt Lydia's. If the two of them joined forces, she'd be doomed.

She grabbed a shawl and wrapped it around her shoulders before going downstairs to the shop. "The days are getting shorter. I miss the light already, and November is only beginning."

Before she could light a lamp, he leaned from behind and whispered in her ear, "You'll think about my offer?" His breath was hot against her neck, and she closed her eyes but nodded. "Good. Then think about this too."

He gently turned her around, cupped her face in his hands, and kissed her. A long, searching kiss, his tongue tracing the seam of her lips, asking for permission. She granted it, her heart pounding as he swept inside her mouth. When he raised his head, her breath came in pants. "Oh, my."

"Should I apologize? I find my restraint sorely tested when I'm with you." He leaned down and nuzzled her ear. "Shall we make plans for the end of the week?"

Genie placed her hands on his chest and pushed back. "You must realize it's hard to think when you're so close." His roguish grin made her laugh.

"Good! I have some effect on you, then." He took her hand and placed it in the crook of his arm and strolled toward the front door of the shop, where the boy and his horse waited.

"I like to stroll through St. James's Park on Saturday afternoons when the weather allows," she told him as they paused at the front door, and he donned his hat. "Perhaps you'd like to accompany me?"

"Nothing could keep me away." With that, he bowed and left her in a puddle of conflicting emotions.

One hand cradled her tumultuous belly. The other touched her lips, where the taste of tea and custard and *him* still lingered.

* * *

CLAYTON TOSSED the lad a coin and told him to return the horse to the livery. He rubbed his side, reluctant to mount with the soreness from his ribs increasing. He'd probably given too much, from the look on the boy's face, but Clayton was in a fine mood. The day had dawned with blood and a promise of more to come. But it was ending with the memory of sweet lips and a soft body against his. Perhaps she was the one who would convince him to don the leg shackles. No one else had ever stirred his blood like Miss Chapelle.

He turned left onto Cannon Street, toward Gracechurch. He would stop by and check on Gus. The fog was already curling out of the alleys, like fingers of a smoky predator slithering along the street, hunting its next victim. The heavy fog smothered him, and Clayton hurried his step to reach the warm household of the O'Briens.

"Get out of da cold, boyo," huffed Paddy when he opened the door. "Just in time for a nip o' whiskey."

"When isn't it time for a nip of whiskey?" Clayton asked with a grin. "How's Gus?"

"He's as cross as a bag of weasels. Grumbling 'bout being confined and poutin' dat Nora stopped doctorin' him."

"Sounds promising." Clayton removed his hat and great-coat, hanging them on a hook in the entryway. Sunday was usually the domestic's day off, so the door was manned by whoever was closest, and visitors took care of their own outerwear.

He headed down the hall, toward the kitchen and the room behind, suddenly anxious to see his friend.

"I'll follow with a decanter," called Paddy from behind him.

The servant's quarters was a tiny room with a narrow bed, set of drawers, and a chair. A pitcher of water and a bowl for washing sat on the dresser. Gus looked like Gulliver strapped down by the Lilliputians. Except for the yards of white linen covering his left shoulder and belly.

"Still breathing, I see?" Relief flowed through Clayton despite his smirk. "What will it take to get rid of you, Rutland?" He settled on the chair next to the bed.

"More than some rag-tag and bobtail." Gus grunted as he adjusted his position in the bed.

"I'm almost surprised to see you still lazing on a mattress." Clayton knew the giant could hide pain well. If he thought he was needed, Gus would be up in a flash, ignoring them all.

"Sampson's concerned with infection, so I'm down for a week. Says that's what makes the flintlock so dangerous, not the lead ball." A grin suddenly split Gus's face.

Paddy stood in the doorway with a decanter in one hand, three glasses clutched between his fingers, and his wrist slid under the slat of a chair. He handed the whiskey to Clayton, then gingerly retrieved the glasses with his free hand and set down the chair.

"Now, we can have a civilized conversation without da women," he said, putting the glasses next to the pitcher and wiggling his fingers for the decanter. "Much pain, boyo?"

Gus grunted again. "Depends on whether I move. But I'll mend as I always do."

"He wouldn't take any more laudanum once he woke. Nora got disgusted, called him a martyr, and took her leave." Paddy took a sip, smacked his lips, and let out a satisfied sigh. "Whiskey, women, and well-doers. They'll—"

"Be the death of us all," chimed in Clayton and Gus. All three laughed and clinked glasses.

"How's Roger?" Clayton still felt guilt creep up his chest when he thought of what he'd dragged the lad into.

"Best call him Lynch now, for he'll be callin' ye Pierce and Rutland. Seems he's been t'rough a wee initiation of sorts." Paddy shook his head. "Da boyo's tough. Knew it when I hired him. If he didn't have a mother, I'd have taken dat one in."

"He played a man's game last night and took the consequences like one. I'm impressed with his skill, but even more, the fact he never got ruffled till it was over." Clayton snorted.

"Perhaps we should send him over to Bow Street? Eli's been there almost two years, and I don't think he'll be staying."

Paddy cleared his throat. "Walters said they already found da body of da rapscallion Roger knocked out. Floatin' in da Thames with his throat slit. That one won't be talkin' to anyone."

"My fault we didn't catch one for questioning," mumbled Gus. "I'll make it right, though."

"Ah, don't be down in da mouth, boyo," admonished Paddy. "It's just da way da cards fell. There'll be more chances. And t'ink of da ones who didn't get away because of ye."

Another clink of glasses.

"So, what of the ones who got away?" Clayton knew the two escapees were injured and would need help. The knife wound in the leg would need stitches, and the other man had been shot.

"Eli's got da Runners on da lookout askin' questions, Walters is checking with his contacts, and you and I'll do the same." Paddy scratched his jaw. "They're dead men walkin', if we don't find 'em first, and joining their silent comrade in da Thames."

* * *

THE NEXT DAY, those words echoed in Clayton's head as he left his home on Threadneedle and made his way to the Stock Exchange Coffee House down the street. It was a favorite haunt of the men since it had good food and was close to both Clayton and Sampson's addresses.

"One down, literally," said Walters, his ruddy face screwed up in thought. He ran a hand over his dark brown curls tipped with silver, sending them in different directions. "And one left to find."

Sir Harry, knighted after his help with the Cato Street Conspiracy, was the first of Paddy's boyos. He could blend into any crowd, and his disguises had even fooled Clayton. His reputation for being deadly with a weapon and always getting his man had led him to cases with the Home Office and members of the peerage. He was, in fact, engaged to the sister of one of the earls he'd worked for.

"Night watchman found him in an alley, knife wound in his thigh. Figured he'd been robbed." He leaned back as their barmaid Sally put tin platters of eggs and cold meat in the center of the table. "Sally, luv, if I didn't have a fiancée, you'd sorely tempt me."

The blonde giggled. "I'll be back with some bread and jam and more coffee unless ye're ready for some ale."

"Some cheese?" asked Sampson.

"Sure," Sally said with a wink and disappeared into the crowd of boisterous patrons.

"What's next?" asked Clayton. "Do we wait for the last man to come out of hiding?"

"I've got a lead that might get me in with the coin counterfeiters. If I do, I'll be able to tail the supervisor, see where he goes, who he talks to." He took a big bite of the eggs, followed it with a slice of ham, and said around the food, "Slow but steady, my friend. Slow but steady."

"You'd think he'd have better manners," Sampson said with a grin. "*Sir Harry* and all."

"It wasn't manners what got me the knighthood. It was my lack of—"

"Humility?" Clayton waggled his eyebrows. "Ability to curse in any brogue?"

"In the meantime," continued Walters, forking a piece of cold roast beef, "why don't ye start on the missing daughter case? Might as well bring in some blunt on something likely to be solved sooner than later."

The men all received a share of the income from Paddy's Investigative Service besides whatever cases they took on the side. Those who did the daily footwork received a percentage, others like Sampson or Benjamin received a flat fee for their service. Sampson performed autopsies that the Home Office or Bow Street wanted to keep quiet and treated injured personnel when needed. Benjamin was the Peeler solicitor, keeping records of the evidence and making cases ready for court.

"The missing by-blow, it is. Just the kind of case I *won't* be needing Dr. Brooks for." Clayton tackled his breakfast with gusto now. "Almost like being on holiday!"

CHAPTER 11

Three days later
Early November

*C*layton let out a ragged sigh. He'd had no luck finding any information on a runaway mother with a daughter. Of course, with a time lapse of twenty-six years, he shouldn't be surprised.

He pushed open the door of Madame Chapelle's, deciding to cheer himself up. He saw the lovely young owner look up from a long counter spread with materials. He recognized one of the patterns from their trip to the linen draper's.

"Oh, Mr. Pierce. What a surprise!" Her amber eyes sparked with what he hoped was pleasure.

"A pleasant one?" he asked with a grin, removing his hat.

"Always," she said with a sunny smile. "What brings you in today?"

"I've had a bit of bad luck with a case, so I said to myself, 'Pierce, what could put a smile back on your face? Why, Miss

Chapelle, of course.' So here I am." He bowed before her and then repeated the motion when her aunt, Mrs. Peckton, emerged from the back room. "And I'm happy to say my *self* was correct." He flashed his white teeth as proof.

Both ladies laughed. "I admit you've also brightened my day," replied Miss Chapelle. "And your eye is somewhat improved."

Clayton reached up and touched the offending bruise with a finger. He'd forgotten about the deuced thing. "Are we still planning on a stroll through St. James's on Saturday?"

"If the weather permits. We may need an alternate plan." Her eyes dropped to his lips, then her cheeks reddened, and she looked away.

"If it's chilly, I'll bring a carriage. We can drive there and avoid a prolonged walk in the cold. Will that suffice?" She was delectable today in a pale-blue muslin gown, even with the moderate neckline. Tiny embroidered birds of brown and a deeper blue seemed to take flight along the hem. "Perhaps Mrs. Peckton would accompany us to prevent any scandals in a closed carriage?"

"I'm happy to come along if needed," said her aunt. "Now if you'll excuse me, I have some hemming to finish." She disappeared behind the curtain into the workroom.

"That's a relief. I'd be right bobbed if we had to cancel altogether."

They spoke of the weather which had resumed its typically cool temperatures. Clayton decided he should leave before he was tempted to kiss her. A customer would surely choose such a moment to enter. So, he bowed over her bare hand, then flipped it, and kissed her palm. He chuckled at her gasp, then stood, and leaned close. "You're invading my dreams, Miss Chapelle. I must ask you to stop, or I won't be responsible the next time we're alone."

"Only if you quit my dreams first," she said in a sassy tone that sent heat spreading through his core. "It seems we're at a stalemate."

His smile faltered, remembering the night at the warehouse when the scalawag had said the same thing, but recovered quickly. "But what a delightful predicament to be in, wouldn't you say?"

With that, he turned on his heel, replaced his hat, and left the shop, whistling.

* * *

SATURDAY

GENIE DONNED the soft gray pelisse of kerseymere. She had tried something different with this design, trimming it with tassels of faux fur which resembled silver fox, copying the old military style from earlier in the century. The pieces were sewn on both ends of the length of fur. She had attached them along the pelisse opening on one side and continued around the hem. A length of thin ribbon of the same gray color was secured beneath the fur and pulled through the velvet cloak. The ribbon, now hiding on the inside of the pelisse, could then be looped around Dorset buttons on the opposite side of the opening, with only the fur tassels showing.

Beneath the hem, her pale-rose walking dress peeked out, covering most of her best leather half boots. Anticipating the brisk day, she wore an extra layer of petticoat, the top layer made of wool. Her hair was twisted under a faux fur cap, and she scooped up the matching muff.

"Oh my. I believe I need a cloak of that style. You outdid yourself, my dear," said Aunt Lydia. "You must have done a good deed to receive this weather today. Cold, but sunshine and no wind." She picked up the hem of Genie's walking dress and nodded in approval at the woolen petticoat.

"Are you sure you won't come?" Genie's eyes traveled down her aunt's muslin day dress and lace cap on her head.

"I've a novel I've been trying to finish. Unless he comes in a closed carriage, you won't need me." She patted Genie's cheek. "Have a splendid time with your handsome young man."

Genie's cheeks burned. "He's certainly not *my* young man."

"Give him time, my dear. Give him time."

And when Mr. Pierce arrived, she wondered if her aunt might be right. She also had to admit her pulse went a bit erratic at the sight of him. His black greatcoat made him look so... hero-like. His auburn curls escaped beneath his beaver hat, and there was a devilish glint in his eyes at odds with the sweet lopsided grin. If the protagonist stepped out of a romance novel, Genie was certain he would look like Mr. Pierce.

"Your eye seems to have healed quickly," she remarked as they left the building.

"Thanks to Nora. When I told her I was taking you to St. James's, she attacked me with her theatrical sponge and dotted away the last of the bruise." He winked at her. "Please, I beg you not to share that information with anyone. Or splash me with water!"

She laughed, her heart light. He helped her into the handsome black curricle hitched to the same team of chestnuts. Before he climbed up to join her, he asked if she preferred the top down. But the sunshine was too inviting, so she declined, and they chatted merrily on their way to the park. Once there, a waiting lad rushed up to handle the horses.

It seemed half of London—the half not at Hyde Park—was promenading on the Mall today. She felt light and young and pretty. "Do you come to the park much, Mr. Pierce?"

He shook his head. "But you come every Saturday? For exercise or to visit with friends?"

"I hate to admit I don't have many friends outside of Aunt Lydia's circle and those connected with the shop. The Saturday strolls are for exercise. I love being outdoors. But also, to see what the ladies are wearing and to show off my latest creation if I have one."

"And is this exquisite pelisse one of those?" He reached across their joined arms to brush a finger over the fur. "Is it real fox?"

She laughed. "No, but you can't tell from a distance. Some of my clientele can afford such luxury, but many can't. They aren't poor, just not as flush in the pocket as the *ton* at Hyde Park."

"Ah, now that's where you're wrong." He deftly moved them between two groups of pedestrians, and they continued down the gravel path. "There are many peers who can't afford to pay their bills. While they may dress finely, they have no more money than many of your clients."

"Very true, sir," she agreed. "I know of more than one modiste who went out of business in Mayfair for that very reason. I'm fortunate to be where I am, right here in Cheapside."

"Were you raised here?" he asked as they moved between two more throngs and ambled along the Mall. "I know Mrs. Peckton has lived here as long as I can remember."

"You make her sound ancient."

"Your aunt visited the O'Briens often," he said with a laugh, "and I remember being amused by some of their conversations. Mrs. Peckton and Maggie are both outspoken women. Now I wonder why you never came with her."

"I think Mrs. O'Brien was Aunt Lydia's refuge. The place she went to get away." Genie nodded at a couple passing, recognizing one of her walking dresses. "I stayed with my mother, of course."

"To think of all the years I've missed of your stimulating company."

"You are flirting, sir. Let's stay on topic." But her fingers gripped his muscular arm a bit tighter. "When my uncle died, Aunt Lydia moved in with us, and they eventually opened the shop." She stepped around a muddy area. "My mother was alone, and I was only a few months old, so it was an ideal venture."

"Was your mother always a seamstress?"

She nodded. "My grandmother worked as one in a small village to the north, and she passed her skills on to both her daughters. When Mama died, I was nineteen. I made an oath to myself that we would make the business one of the most successful in Cheapside."

"Madame Chapelle's has an excellent reputation, so I believe you've succeeded."

"It's kind of you to say. Or have you been investigating me?" she teased.

"Blast! You've found me out."

"So, you've discovered my true identity?" She gasped and put the back of her hand to her forehead. "I suppose this means my days working as an English spy are over. Or did you find out about my life as an acrobat in the traveling circus?"

"The first is much too dangerous for such a demure lady, though your skill with a needle might come in handy."

"Yes, I could sew a criminal's trouser pants together so he cannot run. Or sew a traitor's lips closed so he never speaks against the Crown." She giggled at the thought.

"Hm, perhaps the lady is not so demure after all.

However, I must admit the second secret identity has put quite an image in my head." He winked and sent a thrumming to her toes. "But fortunately, you have another line of work to fall back on which is neither so gruesome nor risqué."

"Now that you know all my secrets, it's your turn. Were you born in Cheapside?"

"Whitehall. My mother died when I was a boy of nine, and Maggie swooped in like an angel. She's been a second mother to me." He studied her for a moment. "I've never admitted this to anyone, but I'm sure my life expectancy improved dramatically once I joined the O'Brien clan. My mother could never have offered me the opportunities they have."

"Fate, I'd say." A warmth spread through her chest at the confidence. "What of your father?"

"Didn't like responsibility much, so he abandoned us when I was born."

"I'm sorry. It must have been difficult for both of you." Genie had never lacked the basic needs in life. "I was lucky. Even without a father, I never went hungry or worried about shelter."

"I can't say I did, either. My ma took good care of me until the fever. But I've always had this secret urge to find my father." He snorted. "And plant him a facer."

"Which he would deserve."

Mr. Pierce stopped and turned to face her. "Thank you."

"For what?" He'd turned so serious.

"For making me feel comfortable enough to confide in you. I'm usually much more reserved."

Oh, those mossy eyes sent chills up her arms. He wouldn't kiss her here, with all these people present. He *couldn't*. Could he? A thrill rippled through her, and then a fat drop of moisture splashed her face. Her first horrifying thought was a bird... Then another. *Plop!* And another.

Rain! When did the sun disappear? "We've been so busy chattering, we didn't notice the clouds."

"What the deuce," mumbled Mr. Pierce, placing his hand on her back and turning them toward the carriage. "London weather! We'll have to make a run for it."

They were soaked by the time they reached the carriage and put the top up. Mr. Pierce tossed the boy a coin that made him smile despite the rain. Genie was thankful for her sturdy pelisse and half boots, but her teeth were chattering by the time they reached Clement's Lane.

He pulled up to the front door of the shop, and she turned to look at him. She burst out laughing, lifting a finger to wipe at the smudge below his eye. "It seems your time on the stage has come to a close."

Mr. Pierce put his finger to his eye and let out a guffaw. "A man of disguise I'm not," he agreed.

"I wish you could stay, but you'll catch your death if you don't get out of those clothes," she said loudly over the drumming of rain on the leather top. "There's Aunt Lydia waiting at the door. I swear she's a mind reader."

When Mr. Pierce helped her down, he kissed her wet glove and wrinkled his nose. "Not the ending I had in mind. We'll have a do-over."

Inside, her aunt fussed and *tsked* over her sodden clothes. She hummed as Aunt Lydia stripped her down and handed her a dressing gown.

"I take it from the sammy smile on your face that you had a nice time?"

"We talked as if we've been friends for ages. He has a way about him which puts me at ease." She chewed her bottom lip. "I've never felt this way."

"You've been bitten, then."

Genie sighed, feeling like a princess in a fairy tale, and twirled in front of the hearth. "Despite the weather and the constant flutters in my belly, I find myself quite enjoying courtship."

Aunt Lydia snorted. "Says the girl who insisted she didn't need romance in her life."

CHAPTER 12

Two weeks later

His case had stalled, which made him even hungrier to find the chit. No one had heard of a woman named Horton. He'd combed every street and alley, spoken to every contact, and come up empty-handed. Clayton had tracked down the previous partner of the solicitor who had issued the payment to Miss Horton. But the man said the building where their office had been burned down years ago. All their files, gone. So, he and his partner had retired rather than start over. Clayton had considered going to see the steward, Mr. Horton—the grandfather of the girl in question. But if he'd disowned his daughters, the cursed man would have little information… unless he had a portrait.

Besides that, Gus was recuperating and out of bed but moving slowly. And in a foul mood. The giant hated when his body let him down, proud of his strength and stature. He was also grumbling again about Nora. Seems she'd found some new beau. Then there was the overenthusiastic Roger Lynch, full of youthful energy, wanting to be on the streets with the Peelers. His shoulder had healed, and the lad would send them all to Bedlam with his fervor. Walters hadn't been heard from in three days, but they were all hopeful he'd infiltrated the counterfeit operation.

The silver lining? The short visit to the modiste shop the previous week had been so beneficial to his mood, that Clayton began dropping in every other day for a few minutes. Miss Chapelle was a breath of fresh air and fast becoming part of his routine.

He hadn't been sure if the lady had been happy about his impromptu visits until he missed one. She'd been delightfully disappointed, telling him it was only because she'd been concerned. Had he been involved in another scuffle? Was he well?

Clayton had wanted to kiss her on the spot. But there had been several ladies ordering clothes at the time. One of the women had been old Mrs. Ober, the landlady from his youth. He'd kept in touch with her over the years. She'd always been kind to him and his mother. Her face had lit up when she realized he was visiting the modiste.

"She's a good 'un, Clayton," Mrs. Ober had said with a sly grin and a pat on his arm. "Yer ma would 'ave liked her."

The landlady was right, of course. Ma would have loved her as he lov—

Where the deuce did that thought come from?

He sobered at the unfinished turn his mind had taken. Granted, he was courting her. Yes, he planned to marry. But the parson's trap was in the future, not even on the docket yet. The little gray cloud of apprehension hovered above his head until he reached Clement's Way. Clayton stopped at the front door, and there was Miss Chapelle, her whiskey-colored eyes brightening his world, and a smile of sunshine which dissolved the fog above him.

Blast, but she's beautiful. Perfect, really. The ridiculous crooked smile broke free, and he was hopping off the curricle, opening the door, and bowing like some regal dandy.

"My, aren't we gallant today," she quipped and gave him a curtsy. "This week, I must pay more attention to the pedestrians and less attention to my handsome escort."

"You had me at *handsome*, my lady." He held out his arm. "Your wish is my command."

She was wearing the same pelisse with the fur tassels. It was an intriguing coat. Last week, she'd received several compliments from passersby. Miss Chapelle had flushed with pleasure. Those who knew her said they'd stop by the shop. Those whom she didn't know had been told of Madame Chapelle's on Clement's Lane. He was impressed with her business acumen.

It was another clear day but colder. He had pulled the top up on the curricle to avoid the chill wind. Clayton liked having this fine lady next to him—on the curricle, strolling the Mall at St. James's, or next to the hearth with a cup of tea. The awkward silences were in the past, and it seemed as if there was never enough time to ask her opinion on all the topics he wanted to discuss.

"You appear deep in thought, Mr. Pierce." Her gentle voice was a welcome interruption. Why think of the lady when she was right there to talk to?

"I was, and I apologize." He deftly guided the curricle around a parked phaeton. "Our strolls have become one of my favorite pastimes. The random questions last week were so entertaining that I've come up with several of my own."

"I think my favorite has been the magic potion query."

"Since you had the best answer, of course," he teased.

"But wouldn't it be a wonderful world if, with only a sip, a person saw the beauty in everyone? No more wallflowers, no more outcasts!"

"Such an optimist. Mine won't be nearly as philanthropical, but they will test your imaginative brain."

"Oooh, tell me!" She clapped her gloved hands. "Look out!"

A dog had dashed from under another carriage, and Clayton pulled back just in time to miss running over the mutt. He let out a loud sigh, then saw the sweet smile on Miss Chapelle's face. "What?" he asked.

"Did you react so quickly over concern for the horses or the dog?"

"Both. It could have injured Paddy's handsome pair, but I've always loved dogs. The O'Briens always had a wolfhound."

"A wolfhound?" Her light-brown eyes were wide. "As in a wolf and a hound mixed?"

Clayton chuckled. "No, as in an Irish wolfhound, bred to chase the wolves off the island. Giant shaggy gray beasts with the patience of a saint."

"They aren't vicious creatures?" Her expression was doubtful.

"Maggie always said the animals were gentle when stroked and fierce if provoked. However, I will say, as boys, we provoked poor Aonarach to the extreme. Never even a growl. They are the mildest-tempered breed I've been around."

"Interesting. I suppose just the size is intimidating enough. Is the name Gaelic?"

"Yes, it means only or one. This particular pup was the only survivor of the litter, hence the name. Paddy and Maggie make regular trips home and bring back the next generation of loyal hound, but it's been a few years since they returned to Ireland. The present Aonarach is getting old, so I predict a visit to the homeland in the near future." He slowed the curricle and parked as close as he could to St. James's. "I'd be surprised if they did not return with another beastie—as Paddy calls them—on their next visit."

"I'd love to meet the future Aonarach too."

Their eyes met, realization in the shared gaze that they were now speaking about the future. If he read those sparkling eyes correctly, she was hoping for a response. An indication he had been thinking of their courtship in that sense.

"I would very much enjoy seeing your expression when you do."

She beamed at him, and he was tempted to reach up and wrap one of her dark-blonde curls around his finger. Instead, he assisted her to the ground, tucked her arm in his, and steered them toward the Mall.

"Do you know why this path is called the Mall?" he asked, beginning their afternoon discussion. The final leaves had fallen from bare branches, littering the walkway. Dappled light flashed the path with reds, golds, and yellows.

"I do. King Charles II named it for the game pall-mall which was popular at the time." She gave him an adorable, smug smile.

"I didn't think you were interested in history," he said, surprised. "Or were you teasing me before and hold tomes of ancient civilization in that lovely head of yours?"

She giggled. "While I don't have an avid interest in history, I am quite fascinated by games. I've watched pall-mall being played here in the summer."

"Ah, good to know. Competitive, are you?"

"Quite," she said. A hound barked ahead, playing with its master and running in circles. "Now, what questions did you come up with?"

"You'll like this one." He realized with a start that he was learning enough about her to know what might amuse her or be of interest. It was both frightening yet calming at the same time. "What animal would you be?"

"Very nice. I'll have to think on it. Does animal include fish, fowl, and insects?"

He snorted. "Insects? As in a butterfly?"

"Any insect, not just the pretty ones."

"Why would anyone want to be an insect?" He was intrigued.

"Take the queen bee. She's surrounded by male admirers and never works. Personally, I would hate that."

"Of course," he agreed with a smirk. "But I think bees are an exception."

"The female spider uses the male for reproductive purposes only. She eats him when she's finished with him." She gave him a wicked smile.

Clayton shivered. "How do you know this?"

"I have been asked to embroider some unique edgings. A vicar's wife who was an avid gardener wanted lady-birds along the hem of her day coat. She said the little spotted beetles ate the pests off her plants and kept them healthy."

"So how exact is your insect art?" he asked, amused.

"My mother had a book with illustrations, so I'm able to work off a sketch or painting. The text is quite interesting, and I remember reading it with my mother. A few times it gave me nightmares."

"Well, I've decided we will exclude insects from the animal query."

"Fair enough. What is your next question?"

"If you were a day of the week, which one would it be?"

"Monday," she said without hesitation.

"Really? Most people hate Mondays. They must resume work after the Sabbath. Domestics usually have their half day on Sundays." He peered down at her. "I would be a Saturday.

The last day of the week, the final chance to finish whatever you've started. And the day to list all your accomplishments throughout the week."

"Admirable."

"Explain your choice, please," he prodded.

"I see Monday as a new beginning each week. What will I accomplish? Who will I see? What opportunities will present themselves?"

"You see Monday as the day of hope." He pondered this for a moment. "You are a fascinating woman, Miss Chapelle."

"Thank you," she said with a blush.

They had taken the lakeside path and now stopped to watch the collection of birds. Gray herons graced the water, along with ducks, geese, and the famous white pelicans.

"The mountain hare."

"What?" he asked, turning his attention back to her.

"The animal I would choose is the mountain hare."

"Because?"

"They are gray in the summer and white in the winter. It's almost like having two halves of yourself. They manage to blend in with their environment, giving them a better chance for survival, and are comfortable in the heat or the cold."

"And they are adorable," added Clayton.

"Indeed!" She laughed, then poked him in the chest. "And you?"

"You'll think I'm dull, but a tiger."

"Oh no, they are beautiful creatures."

And so are you, he thought. "They are hunters, stalking their prey with patience and cunning. As I like to think of myself when I'm on a case. While they're known for their ferociousness and skill at hunting, they do not kill randomly. Only for survival."

"If only our society was more like the tiger," she murmured.

99

"Exactly!"

They turned back toward the direction of the carriage, making their way past groups also enjoying the clear day. He was surprised at how many of those they passed knew her when he had only met the lady weeks ago. She was gracious, polite, and well received by all levels of people. That, of course, was what he liked about St. James's Park. It was such a hodgepodge of social classes, so much more interesting than the parade at Hyde Park.

The same boy from their first rainy stroll had met them the past two Saturdays to handle the horses. "Here you are, Scottie," Clayton said as he tossed the boy the usual coin.

"Me ma said to be sure to thank ye for her too, sir." The slender blond dipped his and ran off.

"You pay him well and know his name?" she asked. "Probably his age too."

He shrugged. "Twelve. I could have been that boy." He felt uncomfortable speaking of the small acts he did for such lads on the street. While he couldn't change the world, he tried to directly pass on at least a bit of his good fortune.

Clayton walked her inside the shop, and when she turned to him, he crooked his arm around her waist and pulled her close. "I thought I would die from the need to do this."

He dipped his head and sipped at her lips, smiling at the sigh that caressed his. As the kiss deepened, his tongue sweeping in to taste remnants of honey and tea, her arms curled around his neck. He lifted his other hand to her collar, fingers stroking the side of the pale, slender column, knuckles lowering to brush the hollow below her chin.

Her breath caught, and he paused to lift his eyes and give her a questioning look. She answered by cupping the back of his head and standing on her toes to press her mouth to his again. Desire roared through him, his hands slipping beneath her pelisse, feeling the warmth of her body through the muslin of her dress. Her fingers threaded his hair, making his scalp tingle and sending a bolt of heat through his core.

When he broke the kiss, he leaned his forehead against hers. "Next Saturday, weather permitting?" he asked. She shook her head, and a quick panic stabbed him.

"I was wondering," Miss Chapelle asked as her fingers ran along his jaw, "if you would mind escorting me to Hyde Park next week?"

"Getting a bit high in the instep, are we?" he teased.

"No! I like to go before Christmastide and again at the beginning of the Season to see what the *ton* are wearing. The fashion magazines are fine to use as a resource, but it's informative to see what adaptations are being made by the modistes in Mayfair."

The thought of strolling along the Serpentine with Miss Chapelle on his arm sent a rush of pride through him. The woman had bewitched him, and he found he enjoyed being charmed.

CHAPTER 13

Monday

*G*enie heard the tinkle of the bell and looked up to see her handsome beau enter the shop. *When had she begun to think of him as such?* She watched as he made his way past several ladies perusing the most recent *La Belle Assemblée,* tipping his hat at them and receiving smiling nods of approval in return.

"Good afternoon, Mr. Pierce. We aren't usually treated to a Monday visit. Is there a special occasion?" Oh, he looked so handsome with his auburn curls tamed just enough to make him presentable. His greatcoat was open, revealing a pale gray coat and a white- and gray-striped waistcoat. His cravat was moderately tied with a silver Celtic griffin pin in the center. A tiny red stone glinted in the half-lion, half-eagle ornament.

The deep green eyes shone with amusement as he gazed moved over her length. "I wanted to see if you looked different on a Monday. If *hope* was something that might be visible on your face or in your eyes. Are you full of anticipation for the week to come?"

She laughed as he studied her with an invisible monocle, squinting like he inspected an important document. "Seeing you certainly tells me the week has started off in a good direction. And I've been busy taking orders and measuring most of the day, so yes."

"I can see it," he whispered. "The subtle curve of your lips, the warm glint in those honey-colored eyes, hair more spun gold than wheat. There's a breathy excitement stirring the pulse at the hollow of your neck."

She cast a frantic gaze at her customers who were pretending not to look at them. Heavens, what this man did to her insides. Genie thought she might melt into a puddle at his feet.

He bowed over her hand, then looked up, and murmured, "Unless it's only your reaction to me?"

She wanted to wipe the smirk off his face and then kiss him senseless. Instead, she refrained from fanning herself as he winked, replaced his hat, and left the shop.

"Oh, my dear, you're flushed," remarked Aunt Lydia, coming from the workroom. "Do you need to sit for a moment?"

Then her eyes caught Mr. Pierce walking past the front window. "Oh, I see. Perhaps a cold cloth to your forehead?"

"Don't even—"

"Ladies, I found that particular lace," her aunt said as she hurried to the group of women. "We can dye it a shade lighter or darker."

Genie escaped to the back room and dipped a cloth into a basin of water and patted her face.

* * *

ON FRIDAY, Mr. Pierce had sent a note apologizing for being unable to meet her for their usual afternoon stroll. It must have been sudden, for he hadn't mentioned any prior engagement on Wednesday when he'd stopped by.

Aunt Lydia had arranged for a carriage from Mr. Derbin, and both women would go to Hyde Park. "It's cold today. I have hot bricks for the carriage. If the same vendor is nearby as last year, we'll buy some cups of negus to warm our insides."

George arrived and placed the wrapped bricks inside the carriage for them. "Ye're lookin' quite fine today, Mrs. Peckton," he mumbled.

The women looked at each other in shock as the driver closed the door. "He's found his tongue at long last!" Genie said with a giggle.

Aunt Lydia wore a pleased smile. "He has indeed."

As they neared the entrance of Hyde Park, her aunt spied the vendor. "Oh, there she is. Monstrous good negus. The woman puts the perfect balance of sugar and lemon in the wine with just a pinch of nutmeg."

"I remember," Genie responded, her eyes straying to carriages already on parade.

"Mr. Lockwood," called her aunt, "be sure to go as slowly as possible while Miss Chapelle is sketching."

"Yes, ma'am," said the older lanky man, sitting straight in his slate livery, silver hair peeking from beneath his hat. He pulled back on the reins and brought the horses to a sedate walk.

Gray clouds hung low in the sky, threatening an early snow. But the temperature was mild despite Aunt Lydia's claim to the contrary. Genie's pencil flew across the page as she observed the passing carriages, pedestrians, and the riders along Rotten Row. She was excited for this coming Season, noting that the wider skirts were indeed being worn and the ladies' hats were more ornately adorned.

There had been a few drops of rain plopping on the leather roof, and as they neared the Serpentine, the carriage came to a halt next to one of the footpaths.

"Sorry, ma'am," called George. "Several conveyances stopped to pull the tops up in case the heavens open up. Should only be a moment."

Genie gave her hand a rest and leaned back to watch some pedestrians just turning onto the footpath next to her carriage. A small group of three couples meandered away from the Serpentine. The gentleman and his female companion in the back drew her attention. He had a certain command to his walk, straight and proper in his dark great-coat. She, on the other hand, wore a pelisse of azure blue, a popular color from last Season. They both appeared to be around her aunt's age and, given their proximity, married. By the way his free hand covered hers, his head bent close to speak, her face looking up to him, they appeared... in love.

And as she continued to watch their interaction, Genie wondered if marriage could be a wonderful union of two people, if a man could look at her that way when she was plump and graying.

The idea warmed her, but as she sat back, an uncharacter-istic foreboding settled over her when another couple entered her peripheral vision. They were not touching, but moving at a more urgent pace, catching up with the group. This man was very tall with a hard, angular face, narrow eyes, and dark mustache. The woman was extremely thin with a large brim to her bonnet, making it hard to see her features. Had they fallen behind their friends?

Just when they caught up with the others, she saw the tall

gentleman take the woman's parasol, as if he was going to open it for her. Instead, his companion stopped, turned in the opposite direction, and began walking away from him with her head down. Her companion moved forward with the parasol, pointing straight out toward the group of pedestrians, aimed at the man in the back.

Is he attacking that sweet couple with an umbrella?

Instead, Genie heard a *click* just as the tall man gained on the couple. Then he swiftly turned, popping open the parasol, and caught up with his companion. They hurried away across the lawn toward a carriage behind Genie. The gentleman in the back of the group was rubbing his neck and looking around. His wife spoke to him. He shook his head, then rubbed his neck again before they resumed their stroll.

How odd! she thought. *Had he been poked with the parasol?* Then the carriage lurched, and the line of conveyances continued forward.

* * *

THURSDAY

GENIE SAT before the crackling fire reading the newspaper. It had been a long day on her feet, and she appreciated the soft footstool, warm hearth, and hot tea. An article with a likeness of a man below it caught her attention.

THE BODY of Lord Major Hatley will be deposited in the family vault, in the Parish Church of St. Mary-le-bone on Friday. He was commended for his bravery and service to the Crown in the Napoleonic Wars and the Hundred Days and christened a Knight Commander of the Most Honorable Military Order of the Bath. He *retired from His Royal Majesty's Army after inheriting his title of Viscount.*

Lady Hatley described her husband as a healthy and fit man. But after a pleasurable walk in Hyde Park on Sunday last, he came down with a chill and succumbed to a fever Tuesday.

SHE STUDIED the sketch of Lord Hatley in his military uniform. Genie's heart pounded as she stared at the face of the man she'd seen last Sunday. The gentleman who had doted on his wife, then turned and looked about, rubbing his neck. She felt sick, and her hands began to shake, the foreboding from that day returning to her chest.

"Aunt Lydia," she called in a high-pitched voice.

Don't panic.

"Yes, dear." Her aunt bustled in with a plate of biscuits and a fresh pot of tea. She set them on the small table between the rockers and pulled her shawl tightly around her shoulders.

"Do you remember me mentioning the strange man with the parasol at Hyde Park?"

"Vaguely, dear. Remind me."

Genie gave a quick summary of the encounter, then handed the newspaper to her aunt. "It's the man who was rubbing his neck. Dead the next day."

"Oh, my," said her aunt. "It's like an espionage novel, but it's real life."

"Are we jumping to conclusions?" asked Genie, chewing on her bottom lip. Her nerves were calmer after sharing her suspicions with Aunt Lydia.

"Let's go over it again. If we do share this information with the authorities, we'll need to have the facts in proper sequence and only tell what you know as fact."

Over the next hour, they discussed the events, going over each detail.

"The lone couple is suspicious, and the viscount had ties to the Crown," summarized Aunt Lydia. "He most likely poked Lord Major Hatley in the back of the neck with the tip of the parasol. Poison?"

"But would that be enough to kill a healthy, robust man?" wondered Genie out loud.

"Shall we call on the O'Briens and see what they think? I believe we have enough to at least suggest foul play."

Genie's stomach clenched. Had she witnessed a murder?

CHAPTER 14

Friday

*C*layton had wanted to stop by Madame Chapelle's, but he'd received a message that afternoon from Maggie to come for dinner. It hadn't been a request. So, he'd finished his business early, skipping his visit, and arrived at the house on Gracechurch promptly at six.

"Good to see ye, boyo," said Paddy, slapping Clayton's back. "Come to da dining room. We will eat before da guests arrive."

"Guests?" Maggie couldn't be playing matchmaker again. Or had Paddy discovered something about one of the cases? He followed the big Irishman down the hall.

They entered the dining room, and he was surprised to see more of the family. Gus and Nora, Sampson and Eli, and Maggie were already seated around the large oak table. He took a seat next to Nora. Gus, of course, was on her other side. "Well, I didn't know it was a family gathering," he quipped, pasting on a smile as the dread slithered up his spine. Something was happening.

"Have we heard from Walters?" *Please, no bad news.*

"He got in and has sent an update," said Eli, the youngest of the boys. His dark-blond hair was short and smoothed back. His blue eyes always shone with optimism. *He would be a Monday,* thought Clayton with a secret smile.

"He'll have to quit that part of the job when he's married," Sampson said, a ridiculous grin on his face.

"Look who's talking of marriage. Is the good doctor still buying sweetmeats from the pretty little costermonger?" Gus snorted with humor when Sampson's face turned red.

"Back to Harry, please?" asked Nora.

"Walters was able to follow the supervisor once after work. They're in a warehouse in the same area in Limehouse. Tonight, he'll do the same. We may finally be getting somewhere." Eli shook his head. "One of the Runners said it's like putting out a blaze with bumpers of water. We only dampen the top layer and never get to the inferno beneath."

Clayton agreed but also knew every man they caught was one fewer criminal on the street. And knowing now that his family was safe—for the time being—he could deal with whatever came next. "But if you don't try, the blaze could take out the whole Town."

"Mrs. Peckton and her niece are stopping by for a visit later," Maggie said casually. "They'll arrive after da shops close."

"A social visit, I hope?"

"Sounded a wee urgent," Paddy said as he settled at the head of the long table.

His gut clenched. "Sounds ominous."

"What could those two ladies possibly be about that

would be ominous?" Nora picked up her glass of wine and held it up. "I have an announcement."

All eyes honed in on Nora, then Gus, then Nora. "Don't look at me," Gus snapped. "I've got nothin' to do with her announcement."

Nora rolled her eyes at the giant's worried look. "I have a role in a play at the Adelphi."

They all cheered and held up their glasses. Clayton tried not to laugh at the relief flooding Gus's face. "What play and who will you be?" Eli asked. "I must be there for your opening night."

"I am Dolly *and* Colombine in *Harlequin in London*." Her green eyes shone with excitement. "If I do well, they may hire me to play in more performances."

"To the future," said Gus, standing. "Our Nora will give the best performance London has ever seen."

Nora stood and toasted with the others, then leaned up on her toes to kiss Gus on the cheek. "Thank you, August."

He mumbled something under his breath at the use of his Christian name.

The meal was served, and Clayton's stomach rumbled. He dipped his spoon into the white soup and made a noise of extreme happiness. "I eat at the best public houses, but none of them compare to home." They passed around the chicken baked in a pastry, spinach and cabbage cake, and mashed turnips.

"How goes the chase, Dr. Brooks?" asked Eli, assuming the innocent look that had saved him so many times as a lad.

Sampson's hazel eyes sent daggers at Eli. "I don't participate in fox hunts."

"I t'ink he means Mrs. Brown," intervened Maggie. "I was planning on asking myself."

The physician's dimples deepened with his smile. He let

out a martyred sigh. "If you must know, I'm getting to know her quite well."

Elijah pushed. "How well? Bann reading well?"

"I haven't thought that far ahead," Sampson said. But he avoided everyone's eyes as he spoke. "She is quite a beauty, though."

He was saved by the arrival of candied pears and minced pie.

They retired to the parlor, the men pouring whiskey and the ladies pouring tea. By eight, the maid announced their guests had arrived.

Clayton stood to meet them, wanting to be sure Miss Chapelle sat beside him. The ladies entered, and he knew immediately something was wrong. Maggie and Mrs. Peckton took the wingback chairs flanking the hearth, with Clayton and Miss Chapelle on the chaise longue facing it. Paddy and Nora brought over two more chairs to complete the circle while Gus, Sampson, and Eli stood behind like guards at the palace gate.

"We believe Genie may have witnessed a crime," began Mrs. Peckton.

"A theft?" asked Paddy.

She shook her head and nodded at Miss Chapelle, who glanced at Clayton. He noticed a slight tremble in her hands and longed to hold them in his own.

"I believe it was a murder."

She began her incredible tale of seeing a man apparently poke a viscount in the neck, pretending to open a parasol. Then the man and parasol quickly fled. The viscount's death had been announced in yesterday's edition of The Times.

"Are you sure the gentleman at Hyde Park is the same as the lord in the newspaper?" asked Gus. "You got a good look at him?"

"Yes, when he rubbed his neck and turned around

looking for the source of the sting or whatever he thought it was." Her amber eyes locked onto Clayton's, fear brightening them. "I could also identify the man with the parasol. I'll never forget his face."

She pulled a sheet of paper from her reticule and unfolded it. "I tried to sketch an image of him, but I'm terrible with faces. I can recreate a fashion to minute detail, but human features are beyond me."

They passed around the drawing. Eli studied it for a long moment. "Miss Chapelle, my talent seems to pick up where yours leaves off. Would you mind if I tried?"

"But you've never seen the man," said Mrs. Peckton.

"Miss Chapelle can begin with what she remembers, then as I draw, she can guide the finer details." He left the parlor and returned with his own pad and a pencil. "Are you ready?"

She nodded, her face already relaxing as she saw the support from everyone in the room. "You believe me, then?"

"Of course," Clayton said.

"We believe ye saw something," said Paddy evenly. "But we must find out *what* dat was exactly. Never fear, Miss Chapelle. We'll get to da bottom of it."

She began describing the man's face, his angular features, the narrow eyes, the hair which had been visible beneath his hat. As Eli sketched, Miss Chapelle made corrections to narrow the chin or widen the forehead. As the face emerged, she gasped. "That's him."

Eli held up the portrait.

"Oh, my. It's like you reached inside my brain and pulled out the image," murmured Miss Chapelle. "Such talent."

"Now we have somewhere to begin," Paddy said with satisfaction.

An hour later, Clayton escorted Miss Chapelle and her aunt to the waiting carriage. "I will stop in tomorrow and see how you fare. I'll understand if you're not up to an outing," he said, leaning inside the carriage, fussing with the carpet over their laps.

"Did I do the right thing?" she asked, a tremor in her voice.

"Yes, and I'm glad you came to us." He'd seen the look in Paddy's eyes. He knew something about this. There'd been a gleam of excitement as the sketch became an actual face.

When he returned to the parlor, Paddy was back in his leather chair by the fire, a glass of whiskey gleaming from the crackling embers. Nora and Maggie had retired. "Boyos, I have some news." His tone said this was business.

Sampson and Eli were on the chaise longue, Gus leaning on the mantel, so Clayton took the other wingback chair. "Does it have something to do with the event in Hyde Park?"

"Aye," he said. "It seems while we've been tracking down *how* the counterfeit notes are being made, da viscount was finding out *where* dey were going. He'd sent a note on Friday last that he had some information but didn't want to put anything on paper. He was to meet an agent Saturday night."

"But he was sick with fever," Eli finished.

Paddy nodded. "He was delirious and died two days later. Never regained consciousness, never was able to tell da agent what he'd discovered."

"Sounds like someone knew what he was up to." Gus began pacing, hands behind his back, a scowl on his handsome face. "The villain on that paper is only a piece of the puzzle."

"But you can't complete da puzzle without every piece," Paddy reminded them. "Here's another. Two more agents who got too close came down with da same terrible fever."

"Poison," Clayton said. "And now we know how."

"But how do we prove it?" asked Eli.

"I need to see those bodies," said Sampson. "I'd wager

there's a common puncture in all three. What was used, I may not be able to tell."

"As a matter of fact, boyo," said Paddy with a grin, "that was my next step. We've already been asked for yer assistance. Da Crown doesn't want anyone knowing da viscount died from anything other than a fever."

CHAPTER 15

*C*layton rose early and met Sampson at the public house on Threadneedle. While they waited for Sally to bring their meal, the men sipped their coffee. The physician told Clayton about the widow he was courting.

"You're using the word courting now?" he teased.

Sampson nodded. "Yes. I'm at sixes and sevens when I'm not with her. I may as well admit it to everyone and move forward." He grinned. "You'll like her. She's beautiful and kind and educated."

"A costermonger?"

"She was an instructor at a girl's school before marrying and coming to London. There's a girl involved, not her daughter, though she's raising the child."

"Sounds like the perfect addition to our family."

"How about you? Have you found the earl's missing daughter? Gus said you'd hit a dead-end." Sampson looked up as the buxom Sally brought their platters. She pushed the cap back on her curly blonde hair. "Can I get you gentlemen anything else?"

"No, ma'am. We thank you." Sampson pushed some coin to the edge of the table. "Keep what's left."

She smiled and left them to their meal.

"The woman and child seem to have vanished once they came to London. I'm even tempted to go to the earl's estate and speak with the steward. He cast his daughter out, but perhaps he kept a miniature of her. Or an image of his wife, who may have looked like her daughter. People may remember a face—" He blew out a loud breath. "I'm grasping at straws."

"Why don't you see if the earl will give a description of the girl's mother to Eli?"

Clayton's mouth dropped. "The deuce if you aren't brilliant." He slapped his hand on the table. "I'm sure Lord Winston would cooperate if it helped locate his daughter."

* * *

GENIE SQUEEZED Mr. Pierce's hand. They stood in the parlor after having tea. "Thank you for understanding," she said quietly, wondering how long this silly fear would last. "I'm just a bit skittish about parks for now."

"You were very brave coming forward," Mr. Pierce said. "Put it out of your mind and know the villain will come to justice."

"If you find him, will I need to testify in court?" The thought terrified her. He must have seen it in her eyes, for he wrapped his arms around her. She sighed into his shoulder, soaking up the strength in his muscled chest.

"Perhaps. But let's not worry about the unknown." He tipped her chin up. "Do you trust me?"

She nodded. *With all my heart,* she cried silently.

He cupped her face in his hands. "Good, then all will be

well." He bent his head and brushed her lips, waiting to see if she responded. Ever the gentleman.

Her arms went around his waist, and she pressed against him. The hardness of his body gave her comfort, and his lips calmed her. He would protect her. She knew it without needing to hear the words spoken.

Her heart whispered to tell him, tell him how much she cared. She wanted to see him every day, longed to know what it would be like to have more than his kisses. Genie realized with a start that she was falling in love with this dear man.

As he held her close, his breath stirring the hair on top of her head, he murmured, "I was wondering if perhaps we could move on from the Mr. and Miss? I would be honored to hear my given name on your lips." He leaned back and studied her.

With a smile, she nodded again. "I agree… Clayton." The small gesture gave her such a thrill. "Please, call me Genie."

"Is Genie a nickname?" he asked.

"My given name is Eugenia, but I've always been called Genie." She took his hand. "Shall I walk you out?"

"I'd be devastated if you didn't."

CLAYTON HAD an appointment in another part of London that afternoon. He was picking Eli up on Bow Street, then meeting Lord Winston at five. An eternal drizzle had settled on the Town the past two days. He preferred horseback, but in this weather, he had given in and rented a hackney. When the carriage pulled up to the Mayfair townhouse, he was lost in thought. *Genie.* A lovely name. He had succumbed to those honey-brown eyes. He wanted more. More time with her, more conversation, more kisses, more—

"Shall we sit in the carriage and gaze at the architecture or go inside and speak with the earl?" asked Eli, a smirk pulling at the corner of his mouth. He picked up his leather folio with his sketch pad.

With a start, Clayton bent his head and peered out at the brick home. "Out with you," he said. "I was just daydreaming a bit."

"I have no doubt. Visions of a lovely blonde damsel in distress with light-brown eyes." Eli batted his lashes. "Save me, Sir Clayton."

"Someone will need to save you if you keep it up," he grumbled as they climbed the stairs.

They waited in a large parlor. The walls were covered with a print silk, Axminster carpets beneath their shoes, and a sparkling chandelier above their heads. The mantel was intricately carved with expensive urns and ivory figurines of jungle beasts placed on top. A curio cabinet held a collection of tea sets, obviously purchased in far-off lands.

"I couldn't begin to imagine how much blunt is sitting in this room," murmured Eli.

"My thoughts exactly."

"Gentlemen," boomed the earl as he entered the room. "Mr. Pierce, it is good to see you again." They shook hands, and Clayton introduced him to Eli.

"Your note intrigued me. But I must warn you, my memory is a bit faded." Lord Winston went to a sideboard. "Would you gentleman care for brandy?"

They nodded, and he poured the liquor into three cut-crystal glasses. After settling in chairs, they began.

"Lord Winston, we'll begin with the basics. Describe the shape of Miss Horton's face, eyes, nose. As I sketch, you can have me adjust width and depth," began Eli. "I have brought some pastels to match the color of her eyes and hair."

The earl nodded and began his description. Twenty

minutes later, Lord Winston jumped from his seat. "Bullocks, that's her. How the deuce did you do it?"

Clayton looked at the face, stunned. He couldn't breathe. It was Genie looking back at him.

"The hair could be a little darker, more the color of wheat in the fall," the earl was saying. He grabbed the sketch pad and stared at it. "I feel like I've gone back to my days at university."

"Good, I'm glad I was able to help," Eli said, taking back the sketch pad and putting it in his portfolio.

"Will this help, then?" Lord Winston's voice cracked. "Do you think we'll find my daughter now?"

Clayton nodded, his mouth numb, unable to form words. He was in love with an earl's daughter. Oh, fate had a vicious sense of humor. Unless by some extraordinary coincidence…

"My lord, may I ask your Christian name?" Clayton's fingers clenched the arms of the chair.

"Eugene. Why?"

Eli rose. "In case your daughter was named in your honor."

Clayton looked up to see Eli standing in front of him, a question in his blue eyes. He put a hand on Clayton's shoulder. "Shall we go?"

Rising, Clayton put out his hand. "Thank you for seeing us, my lord."

"My pleasure, Pierce. This has been an entertaining afternoon."

Somehow, he found himself in the hackney, staring blindly out the rain-streaked window. He leaned his head back on the hard leather squabs.

"What the devil happened in there? You look like you've seen a ghost." Eli sat on the opposite bench. "Clayton, talk to me."

"That sketch is almost a perfect image of Miss Chapelle." His tone was flat, like his heart.

"*Your* Miss Chapelle?" Eli took out the sketch, then whistled. "I knew the features were familiar, but are you sure?"

Clayton shook his head. "Her given name is Eugenia."

"Oh."

"But if she's a by-blow, what difference—"

"She carries the blood of a peer in her veins. I'm a commoner from Whitehall, for God's sake." He threw his hat on the seat and ran a hand through his hair. "It's a chasm too wide to cross, regardless of what side of the blanket she was born on."

The hackney bumped along, jarring both men into a gloomy silence.

"I thought she was half French?" Eli looked at the face again. "What do you know about her father?"

He shook his head. "We never discussed it. When she spoke of her past, she never mentioned a father. I assumed he died or…" *Abandoned them like his own father.* He hadn't given it much thought because her origins hadn't mattered to him.

"Clayton, how many times have you met someone that you swear looks like someone else you know?"

He looked at Eli, grasping the ring held out to him. "And Eugene isn't an unusual name."

"No," his brother agreed. "I believe your next move should be asking the lady herself. Either way, at least one man will be happy with the outcome."

CHAPTER 16

*C*layton stretched his tired limbs and yawned. He blinked, his lids like sand against his eyes. He'd barely slept. This morning he would send a note to say he would visit at nine o'clock. He'd ask Genie—no, he couldn't use her given name now—about her father, about her past. If she wasn't Winston's daughter... Eli had given him a sliver of hope, and he'd clung to it during the long hours before dawn.

If this worked out, what would he do? Propose? Tell her how his heart had cracked when he thought there had been no chance for them to share a life together? Perhaps it was a sign, and fate was nudging him rather than playing a cruel joke.

Yes, he decided, as he walked toward Clement's Lane. He would ask her to be his wife. Though he hadn't known her long, they suited. Suited?

Admit it, nodcock. Tell her it's love.

He took in a deep breath of the cold, crisp air to clear his head. The chill against his skin was invigorating, refreshing his mind after a sleepless night.

As he passed St. Clement's Church, he stopped. Craning

his neck to peer at the steeple, he considered praying. Clayton had never been a godly man, but if it would help him win this beautiful woman who had stolen his heart, he would gladly fall to his knees.

Lord, you've taken from me, and you've given back more. But I've never asked for your goodness. If I'm allowed one request, let it be her.

He raised his chin and crossed the street. Gen—Miss Chapelle was inside the shop, dressed in a pale-blue muslin, her golden hair loose about her shoulders. She seemed to sense his presence, for she turned, and they locked eyes.

Clayton hurried across the street as she rushed to the door. The bell tinkled when she opened it, smiling.

"Clayton, your note seemed so urgent." She paused, taking in his expression. "What is it? Is someone hurt?"

He shook his head, unable to speak. Fear and hope clogged his throat.

"Come in. We have tea brewing upstairs."

He followed her through the workroom, watching her hips sway as she took each step.

"Have you eaten?" she asked over her shoulder.

"No," he croaked. His fingers twitched to reach out and touch the thick curls covering her shoulders.

When they were in the parlor, she sat in one of the rockers. He paced the floor, wondering how to begin.

"Clayton, you're frightening me. Please, tell me why you've come."

Her whiskey-colored eyes pleaded with him, and he stopped, squatting next to her.

"Who was your father?"

She tipped her head, confused. "My father? I never met him. Mama said he wanted nothing to do with us, so it was better not to speak of it. She said the same of my grandfather." Her eyes narrowed, and anger flashed in them. "Is this because I'm not truly half French? Because I'm… my mother was never married?"

Bloody hell! He was going about this all wrong. "No, no." He grabbed one of her hands, kissing her fingers, then her palm. "I may have found your…"

He stood again and resumed his pacing.

"My what? My father?" She stood and placed a hand on his chest, halting his movement. "Why are you acting so strangely?"

He focused on the mantel over her shoulder—and saw it. One of the miniatures. Why had he never spotted it before? He was an investigator, a man whose livelihood was details. Unless his heart was involved.

"Is that your mother?"

She turned with a smile and picked up the frame. "Yes. I resemble her, don't you think?"

Clayton could only nod. Eli had done an excellent job creating the sketch. It was almost a copy of the miniature.

"Your father—"

"Good morning, to you," called Mrs. Peckton cheerily. She set the tea tray on the table and turned toward them, her smile fading as she took in their countenance.

He cleared his throat. "Ma'am, may I ask what your maiden name is?"

The woman looked taken aback.

"Horton," Miss Chapelle supplied for her aunt.

He sank down into a chair in front of the tea tray.

"I think it's time you stopped being so mysterious, young man," said Mrs. Peckton as she poured tea for all of them. "Genie, come sit by him."

Where to start? At the beginning, he supposed. By the time he finished, Miss Chapelle looked stunned, but her aunt was furious.

"How dare that pompous addlepate come looking for her

now. It's been… over a quarter of a century, mind you." She huffed. "And now he has a conscience?"

"You knew all this?" Miss Chapelle turned a horrified gaze to her aunt.

"Of course. Marianne was my sister. We grew up with the little toad."

"He did seem sincere, along with his wife," said Clayton. "He truly wants to help. Lady Winston hopes to bring Genie —Miss Chap—" He stuttered to a stop.

"Exactly!" she cried, wiping furiously at the tears rolling down her cheeks. "What should you call me now? Genie is the only *legitimate* name I have."

Clayton couldn't stand the tears. He wrapped an arm around her shoulder and pulled her close. Her cheek was warm and wet, and he suddenly wondered how he could possibly give her up. "Mrs. Peckton, please remember he had no idea he was a father until he became the earl. We don't know what he might have done if he'd known."

The older woman gave an indelicate snort. "It doesn't matter. He can jump in the Thames, along with my self-righteous father, for all we care. We've done just fine on our own."

He kissed the top of Genie's head. "Will you meet him? He insists there will be no pressure. The decision is yours."

She sniffed. "I have siblings?"

He nodded. A ray of hope bloomed inside him. If she didn't embrace her newfound family, perhaps there was still a chance for them. She would not be part of that elite circle, and her life would continue as it had. Yet, he could not influence her decision.

Genie shook her head. "It's too much. I need time to think."

"Of course," agreed Clayton, "I've given you quite a shock. I'll leave you—"

"No!" Genie grabbed his hand, her blue eyes dark with tears. "Please don't go. The only thing I'm certain of is the life I've known. I'm happy here with the family I've known and… you."

His eyes raked over her face, his heart pounding at what she hinted. "I'll stay for a while longer."

"I'll get us something to eat. We can't face a day like this without something in our stomachs," exclaimed Mrs. Peckton, hurrying from the room.

As soon as she disappeared around the corner, Genie laid a hand on his cheek and kissed him. A kiss which held her fear, her hope, her love. Confound it, how he could feel that love.

"Since I met you, I've finally felt as if there is a future for me. Outside of the shop. A place where I belong." She kissed him again, her fingers raking the thick curls back from his temple. Her eyes searched his face. "Don't let this spoil what has grown between us."

He pulled her close, torn between kissing her senseless and begging her to turn her back on her father, or walking away and allowing her to choose her own path.

Then his mouth worked without a prompt, and he heard himself saying, "Whatever happens in the future, know that I love you and want what is best for you."

This time, her tears fell upon her smiling lips, and she kissed him again. "I never thought I would find love. Never worried about it. I kept busy and had a goal. And then you came along, and I realized this special kind of caring is what had been missing."

"Genie, I—"

She put a finger on his lips. "No, let me finish. There was always this empty space inside that I couldn't quite fill, didn't know how to fill. The first time you kissed me, the hollowness disappeared." She shook her head. "You made me whole."

Mrs. Peckton reemerged with another tray. "Homemade strawberry preserves can fix just about anything." There was toast, hunks of cheese, and a bowl of the preserves. "Eat up."

While they munched and drank more tea, Clayton asked, "If your mother never married, how did you come by the name Chapelle?"

Genie laughed, and the sound was a salve for his battered heart. "Chapelle is church in French, and we had just moved here, across from St. Clement's Church. She decided to be a widow and needed a name someone wouldn't recognize."

"People assumed her husband was French because of it," added Mrs. Peckton. "We decided there was no need to dissuade anyone of the idea since it helped business. The gossipmongers took care of the rest."

A chuckle bubbled up from Clayton's chest, thinking of his prayer before the church earlier that morning. "Miss Church," he said, laughing.

Before he left, Clayton promised to stop by on Tuesday. Genie assured him she would decide by then if she wanted to meet her father. He would notify Lord Winston of Marianne's death and his daughter's status.

He walked away from Madame Chapelle's, knowing his own future happiness would hang in the balance for the next forty-eight hours.

CHAPTER 17

*O*onday. What had she told Clayton? Monday was a day of new beginnings. Was it a sign that she should agree to meet the earl? Perhaps. Would he wish her to take his name? If she were to have a new one, Genie only wanted one. Pierce. Genie Pierce. *Mrs. Clayton Pierce.*

But as the day went on, Genie realized perhaps she wasn't ready for any great changes. Only small ones. Coming to a decision, she sat down after dinner to write a letter. It always helped to put words to paper. It helped make sense of her thoughts. It took over an hour, but she was finally satisfied as she reread it.

DEAR LORD WINSTON,

I have received the news of our apparent blood bond. First, I'd like you to know I appreciate the fact you have searched for me. It demonstrates you have integrity. I hold no grudge against you or my mother for the circumstances of my birth.

Mr. Pierce has informed me that you would like to meet. I have reservations, of course. While I am content with my life, I am curious about the family I've never known. Therefore, I believe a slow transition through letters would be a fitting way to become acquainted. It will allow us to ask questions and give honest answers which may be difficult to say when face to face.

By nurturing our relationship in this way, we can come to a mutual agreement as to when we may meet. In addition, I am happy to answer any correspondence from Lady Winston or your children.

If we never meet, please know I am happy and have always been well cared for. There is nothing I want for, and nothing I would ask of you.

Your daughter,
   Eugenia

GENIE HAD STRUGGLED on the signature. It felt odd to use *Chapelle*, yet she could not presume the use of his family name. In truth, she didn't know it. Folding the missive, she addressed the envelope and brought it down to the shop, where she would give it to Clayton on the morrow.

But the next day, Clayton was distant. Genie tried to get him to smile, to tell her when they would have another outing. When he hesitated, the anger began a slow burn in her belly. It couldn't be the circumstances of her birth. Though his mother had been married when he was born, his father had abandoned them. Surely, their situations weren't so different.

On Wednesday, she received a reply from both the earl and the countess. Her father was apologetic and agreed to whatever she thought best. His wife's response was full of warmth and welcome, and from the countess's words, she knew Lady Winston was a kind woman.

By Thursday, Genie wasn't mad, she was furious. How dare he ignore her. They had grown close—no, more than that. He'd said he loved her. Is this how he treated someone he loved? Well, she'd find out.

"Aunt Lydia, I'm going out." They were in the kitchen, and her aunt was putting together a meat pie. "There is something I must see to."

"What? We haven't had dinner yet. Where are you off to?" She wiped her hands on her apron. "Can I do anything?"

"I'm going to the O'Briens. They will know where I can find Mr. Pierce." She had already donned her pelisse and was tying her bonnet. "I will not be ignored. You don't declare your affection for a woman and then… and then… vanish!"

"No, you don't. Go, my dear. Give him an earful!" Aunt Lydia followed her down the stairs. "Shall I send for a carriage to meet you on Gracechurch Street?"

"Yes, please. It's not a long walk to the O'Briens, but I have no idea where Clayton lives."

She checked her reticule, making sure she had money for the driver, and stomped out of the shop.

* * *

CLAYTON SAT in the parlor with Paddy and Walters. Eli's sketch had been a tremendous boon to the case.

"Once I saw that face," said Walters, scratching at the dark stubble on his jaw, "I knew I had to find out what the supervisor looked like beneath his beard. We've got his direction, and we know he's the bugger who killed the Lord Major."

"What we don't know is why," mused Paddy. He took a sip

of his whiskey. "Good work, Harry. Our hunch was right, and the barrels are packed with gunpowder. I'll go to Bow Street tomorrow, tell them which warehouse to find the contraband, and speak to the magistrate about our clever assassin."

"The Vicar loses another important soldier in his war. Who knows? We may get lucky, and the villain will talk," said Clayton.

"And a nice pile of blunt," added Walters. "What did Sampson find from the autopsies?"

"All three had a puncture mark. He doesn't know what type of poison." Clayton shook his head. "It couldn't have been a pleasant way to go." He looked out the window. It had been a good day, but a terrible week. He'd avoided Genie after the earl had said she had agreed to get to know them. The relationship might begin with correspondence, but he had no doubt she would be united with Winston and his family.

"I'm proud of my boyos," said Paddy, grinning. "Two cases closed this week. It'll be a pretty pence for us."

"The murders are solved, but we still have work to do on the counterfeiting," Clayton reminded them.

Walters' dark-chocolate eyes glinted, reflecting his smile. "If you're satisfied with my findings, I have a lovely lady who has been waiting patiently to hear from me."

"I bet ye do, Harry." Paddy laughed. "Ye don't have time for a drink?"

He shrugged. "Ye might persuade me to have one."

They heard someone at the door, female voices murmuring, then the parlor door burst open. Clayton looked up and saw Genie, hands on her hips and fire in her eyes. He swallowed.

"Mr. Clayton Pierce, may I have a word?" she asked

crisply. Without waiting, she strode across the wine-colored carpet and glared down at him.

He immediately stood, hearing a snicker from Paddy and his brother. "I'm sorry I haven't—"

"Oh, I'm expecting an apology, but first, I want an explanation." She untied her bonnet and tossed it on the chair where Clayton had been sitting. Her wheat-blonde curls tumbled about her face, and his fingers itched to pull one.

The anger in her eyes only stoked his desire, and he realized how much he had missed her the past few days.

"How dare you play with my affections, make me believe you love me, and then vanish like that!" She snapped her fingers under his nose. "I trusted you, admitted my feelings, then you tucked it all away in your pocket and left me?"

"Miss Chapelle," he said, then realized when her eyes widened what the mistake he'd made. "I mean, Genie, I didn't want to influence your decision. If you chose to become part of your father's world, I couldn't hold you back."

"Hold me back? Why not stand beside me?" She poked his chest with her finger. "Support me." She poked him again. "What does my father have to do with us?"

"Genie, I'm a commoner from Whitehall," he said in a soothing tone. "We couldn't be together in that world. The London *ton* wouldn't accept me."

"And they'd welcome me? This is about whether I have a relationship with the man who gave me life, not about entering society."

Walters cleared his throat. Genie looked at him askance, as if she hadn't realized there were others in the room. "I beg your pardon, sir, Mr. O'Brien." But her gaze and ire returned to Clayton.

"If I may add a word," Walters continued, his voice growing hard, "are ye saying, Brother, since I'm from the rookery that I'm not fit for Lady Matilda?"

Clayton blinked. *Blast! What had he been thinking?*

Genie folded her arms and gave him a smirk. "See? Even your brother agrees with me. Mr. O'Brien, do you have an opinion?"

"Aye," said the big Irishman with a grin. He turned to Clayton. "The only way I can see a way out of this is to kiss her. And ye better be quick, or it'll be putting out a blaze with bumpers of water."

When the men deserted him, he turned back to Genie. "You're right," he said.

"Of course I am!"

"And so is Paddy," he said, taking a step toward her, a new determination set on his face. "You're mine, Genie. I knew it the first time I laid eyes on you. I've lived on instinct most of my life, and I almost didn't listen to my gut."

He took another step toward her, his eyes narrowed, and this time she took a step back. "Now it's time for you to listen to me." Another step forward, and a step back for Genie. Her expression had changed from anger to wariness.

"I don't care if your father is titled or a petty thief." Another step forward, and another step back for Genie, her eyes wide. "You will be my wife, and we will have a family."

This time when he took a step forward, he grabbed her wrist, so she remained rooted. "If I don't, I'll have Walters and his fiancée to answer to. Besides regretting it the rest of my days."

He pulled her to him, breathed in her scent, and kissed her. Her lips were soft and sweet, her tongue tasted like strawberry preserves, and her body molded to his. When he raised his head, she was panting but smiling. "Any questions, Genie?"

She nodded. "May I have another kiss?"

This time he kissed her like a starving man, and she responded with the wantonness of a woman in love. He feathered kisses along her jaw, nipped her earlobe, and moved his lips along her slender neck. "Shall I apologize now?" he whispered.

"I believe more explanation is needed." Her fingers threaded the hair at the back of his neck, and she reached up to claim another kiss.

THE VICAR

The Vicar ran a hand through his raven hair, ebony eyes glinting with anger through the black satin mask, then slammed his fist on the polished oak desk. But it was his silky smooth voice that sent a chill down Alberts's spine.

"First, the Crown removes the Duke of Colvin from my resources. Next, Bow Street takes Dunn, my best man in the rookeries." The Vicar glared at his minion. "If we are connected to the dead viscount, *you* will be the next victim."

"Yes, sir. I mean, no, sir. Nothing can be traced back to us." Sweat trickled down his back. "The gunpowder has been moved to another location. The barrels were put into boxes, so they won't be easily recognized."

"Everything was going smoothly until..." The Vicar tapped long graceful fingers against the gleaming wood. "We need to find out who the Crown has joined forces with. It's not the Runners. They've brought in someone else."

"I'll see what I can find out." Alberts couldn't wait to get out of there. His gang was dwindling.

"I'm not an evil man, just driven," said The Vicar. "Don't I take care of the widows? I'm generous with my chosen charities. I've done good deeds in the rookeries."

Alberts froze. Was the man actually trying to rationalize his wickedness? Did he forget how it had been his orders that had made those women widows to begin with? Alberts's had hated disposing of Ferguson's wife, but The Vicar's orders had been clear, and Alberts was no fool. It had been the woman or himself. It still roiled his gut when he thought of the little girl who had witnessed the mugging gone wrong. At least, that's how the Runners had reported it.

Ferguson had wanted out, and the man knew too much. The idiot man hadn't believed Alberts would go with through with his threat. By the time the fool had realized it, it was too late. As Ferguson's son was hanged along with Dunn, Ferguson himself had been dumped in the Thames.

Alberts shuddered, thinking of that night. They'd tortured him, trying to change his mind. Threatened to take his daughter, though the chit had disappeared. But Alberts would find her, along with whoever was disrupting the Congregation. It was a shame that Thorton had gone too far in his "persuasion" of Ferguson. However, the man—all the men who joined The Congregation—knew the risks. Greed usually overtook caution, especially the wages offered by the Vicar.

For tonight, he would go home to his sweet daughter Clara, who would have a hot meal waiting for him. Alberts had a sudden urge to envelop her in a ferocious hug. Perhaps he'd buy her a sweet treat on the way home. Tomorrow would be soon enough to think about this gory business.

EPILOGUE

May 1821
St. Clement's Church

"*I* now pronounce you man and wife," the vicar announced to the congregation.

Clayton bent and kissed her, his eyes telling her there was so much more to come.

"Congratulations!" The cries echoed in St. Clement's Church as they departed the building. The people who loved her most enveloped her on both sides of the aisle with their well-wishes. Genie's face hurt from smiling so much. Aunt Lydia was crying, George Lockwood patting her shoulder. Maggie and Nora were wiping away tears. Paddy, Benjamin, and Gus were grinning. Harry and Sampson were both there with their wives.

She'd labored for weeks on her dress of the palest rose; the intricate ivory lace overlay so delicate she'd been afraid to touch it at first. The lace had come from Italy, a gift from her father and Lady Winston. After months of correspondence, they had finally met face to face. With Clayton by her side. She had met her siblings briefly, and they had plans to gather at her brother's estate over the summer months. Neither Genie nor Aunt Lydia wanted to visit Lord Winston's property. Meeting her grandfather would probably never happen, but she was full of joy this day and wouldn't let him cast a cloud.

Clayton wore the silly lopsided grin again. He was so handsome in his slate coattails, his auburn curls barely tamed, and his moss-green eyes dark with desire—and love. It would be an eternity before they finished the wedding breakfast and began their new life with a trip to Paris.

She picked up her skirts, careful of the overlay, and laughed at the worn shoe thrown by Eli as she stepped over it. A sign of good luck that Mr. and Mrs. Pierce hopefully wouldn't need.

"My darling girl," her father said with a laugh as hugged her, "you are stunning. I am so happy for you."

"You make a beautiful couple, my dear Mrs. Pierce," added Lady Winston. "And don't forget, we've arranged for the hotel in Paris—no argument. It's your wedding present."

"But this lace was my wedding present," she reminded them both.

Her stepmother kissed her cheek. "That was for you. The hotel is for both of you."

Clayton dodged another old shoe thrown by Roger.

"May ye have a dram of the happiness I've had with my Maggie," Paddy said, hugging them both, then kissing his wife on the mouth with a loud smack.

"Then we'll be drunk with love," Genie said, squeezing Clayton's hand. Her world had turned upside down and was righted again. With the help of her family—by blood and choice.

"I thought it quite clever how I arranged the wedding on a *Monday*," Clayton said as they settled in the carriage. "New beginnings, Wife." He kissed her soundly, a promise of what was to come later.

TO MY READERS:

THE VICAR IS A RECURRING villain that will appear in each mystery—until he's caught in the final book.

I chose to write a series that included a cast outside the *ton* and set in Cheapside. It is a fascinating district that is not given enough credit for its bustling trade and variety of goods and services at reasonable prices. Here the wealthy merchants mixed with middle and lower classes, enjoying much the same lifestyle as our usual Regency heroes and heroines but in a less lavish background.

REVIEWS ARE the lifeblood of authors. If you've enjoyed this story, please consider leaving a few words at your favorite retailer.

Keep updated on future releases, exclusive excerpts, and prizes by following my newsletter:

https://www.subscribepage.com/k3f1z5

AUTHOR'S NOTE

As my readers know, I always try to mix my stories with authentic places and real historical events. Here are some of the fun facts from this book:

Aonarach, the Irish wolfhound

The Irish wolfhound in this series is based on my own wolfhound, Solo. He was the only pup of his litter to survive. He overcame several major health issues, including gangrene in his tail that was docked. We received this big galoot at six months because he was pet quality and not eligible for the show ring. We didn't care. The name Aonarach (Ay-nuh-rok) means "only" in Irish Gaelic.

Poisons

As I was plotting this story, I researched the possible deadly poisons available during the Regency. I wanted something that wouldn't be recognizable at the time. When I discovered ricin, I hit the jackpot. It is a poison found naturally in castor beans and has been used in South American countries for centuries. The conquistadors of the sixteenth century learned of the poison when the natives attacked with ricin-tipped arrows. If chewed and swallowed, it can kill a person or animal in two to three days, shutting down the liver and kidneys. If injected, it causes a high fever first, then the organs shut down. It is said to be six thousand times more poisonous than cyanide.

I used the parasol theme to commit the murder in Hyde Park. I wanted to use a dart-like ejection, but then the evidence would have been in the victim's neck, eliminating the mysterious death. Much to my surprise—after writing this—I found this exact method was used in the modern assassination of Bulgarian dissident Georgi Markov. The incident occurred on Waterloo Bridge, London, using an umbrella to fire a small pellet of ricin into the victim's leg. He was dead four days later.

In the twenty-first century, the poison has been produced and used for vicarious purposes, including arrests made for its production in the U.S. and England, a terrorist plot in Cologne, Germany, and tainted packages sent through the mail to Washington D.C.

ABOUT AUBREY WYNNE

USA Today Bestselling author Aubrey Wynne resides in the Midwest with her husband, dogs, horses, mule, and barn cats. Obsessions include wine, history, travel, trail riding, and all things Christmas. Her Chicago Christmas series has received multiple awards and was twice nominated as a Rone finalist by InD'tale Magazine.

Aubrey's first love is medieval romance but after dipping her toe in the Regency period in 2018 with the *Wicked Earls' Club*, she was smitten. This inspired her spin-off series *Once Upon a Widow* and the Scottish Regency series *A MacNaughton Castle Romance* with Dragonblade Novels. In 2024, Aubrey will launch Paddy's Peelers, a Regency detective series.

Social Media Links:
  Website:
  http://www.aubreywynne.com
  Facebook:
  https://www.facebook.com/magnificentvalor
  Aubrey's Ever After Facebook group:

https://www.facebook.com/groups/
AubreyWynnesEverAfters/

Twitter:

https://twitter.com/Aubreywynne51

Pinterest:

https://www.pinterest.com/aubreywynne51/

Instagram:

https://www.instagram.com/Aubreywynne51

Bookbub page:

https://www.bookbub.com/profile/aubrey-wynne

Goodreads:

https://www.goodreads.com/author/show/7383937.
Aubrey_Wynne

Sign up for my newsletter and don't miss future releases
https://www.subscribepage.com/k3f1z5

ALSO BY AUBREY WYNNE

Once Upon a Widow series

Earl of Sunderland #1

Maggie award, International Digital Awards finalist

Christopher Roker inherited the title of rake. She hides behind her independence. Fate accepts the challenge…

Escaping his late brother's memory, Lady Grace is a welcome distraction. But as the attraction grows, Kit finds himself wavering between his old military life and the lure of an exceptional but unwilling woman.

A Wicked Earl's Widow #2

Recommended by InD'tale Magazine

Eliza, Lady Sunderland, is widowed after one year. Her abusive father, near financial ruin, is already planning another wedding.

When Viscount Pendleton discovers a beauty defending an elderly woman against ruffians, he is smitten. But Nate soon realizes he must discover Eliza's dark past to save the woman he loves.

Rhapsody and Rebellion #3

Maggie finalist, nominated for Rone Award, InD'tale Magazine

A Scottish legacy… A political rebellion… Two hearts destined to meet…

Alisabeth was betrothed from the cradle. At seventeen, she marries her best friend and finds happiness if not passion. In less than a year, a political rebellion makes her a widow. The handsome English earl arrives a month later and rouses her desire and a terrible guilt.

Crossing the border into Scotland, Gideon finds his predictable world turned upside down. Folklore, legend, and political unrest intertwine with an unexpected attraction to a feisty Highland beauty. When the earl learns of an English plot to stir the Scots into rebellion, he must choose his country or save the clan and the woman who stirs his soul.

Earl of Darby #4

Holt Medallion Winner, NTRWA Reader's Choice Award, Nominated for Rone Award, InD'tale magazine

Miss Hannah Pendleton, nursing her pride after her childhood crush falls in love with another, hurls herself into the excitement of a first season.

Since his wife's suicide on their wedding night, the Earl of Darby has carefully cultivated his rakish reputation. But when Nicholas sees a lovely newcomer being courted by the devil himself, her innocence and candor revive the chivalry buried deep in his soul.

Earl of Brecken #5

He's on the brink of ruin. She's in search of a hero.

Notorious for his seductive charm, the Earl of Brecken searches for a wealthy heiress. His choices are dismal until he meets Miss Franklin. Guileless, gorgeous and with an enormous dowry, she seems the answer to his prayers. Until his conscience makes an unexpected appearance.

Earl of Griffith #6

Sorrow and Regrets…

After eloping, a widowed Lady Helen is disillusioned with love and raising a three-year-old alone. Now she must face the music and her family.

An unexpected ray of sunshine…

Conway, Earl of Griffith is smitten at first sight with his friend's sister and adorable daughter. But can he convince the grieving and lovely widow that love is worth a second chance?

Beware A Wallflower's Wrath #7

Annis Craigg gave her heart—and innocence—away at seventeen.

When Lord Robert Harding returns to Scotland fifteen years later, he's desperate to find the only woman he's ever loved. But she has secrets and an attitude.

Lies, secrets, and betrayal will challenge the fierce love of a steadfast Highlander and remorseful but determined Englishman. Will destiny find a way to bring two star-crossed souls together?

A Wallflower's Wassail Punch #8

Lady Annette's first Season was a disaster after a duke's son pinched her by the punchbowl, and she walloped him in the nose. Five years of malicious rumors later, her father offers an outrageous dowry so he too can marry.

Lord Wilkinson, a widower, meets a striking, intelligent woman, with a dry wit only he seems to appreciate. His heart stirs for the first time in decades. But will their age difference and wagging tongues interfere with their budding romance?

The Scoundrel's Christmas Challenge #9

A contest to win her fortune...

Lady Winfield, a long-time wealthy widow, is infamous for her outrageous house parties. While hosting her annual Christmastide gathering, Christiana proposes a new game: a daily challenge of her choice. She will accept the proposal of the man who can best her at three or more competitions by Twelfth Night. Though all agree to the diversion, no one expects the games to include marksmanship, archery, and fencing.

A contest to win her heart...

When Lucius, Viscount Bolingbroke presents Lady Winfield with a secret challenge, she can't resist. Will their midnight rendezvous and private contests end in certain victory for one or a dual attraction for both?

The Duplicate Duke #10

In a country far, far away...

Lady Gwendolyn Beaumaris and her brother have been known as

the Downing twins since their father's death when they were eight years old. Fearful that their grandfather, the Duke of Shackerley, would take her son, Gwen's mother relocates them to Boston where she has family. Now twenty-two, Gwen has been waiting to hear from her brother who is trying to make his fortune in the fur trade. Down to her last pennies, she must consider a proposal from a wealthy middle-aged merchant who has come to her rescue.

The brass ring is within reach...

Lord Wickton has worked tirelessly the past two years to bring honor back to the family name. His father's debts have been paid, but now he needs the funds to restore the entailed estate to its previous glory. When the viscount learns he is the heir presumptive to his great uncle's dukedom, his prayers are answered. Sending out the obligatory investigators, he travels to Shackerley House to inspect his future inheritance.

A comedy of errors...

When a letter arrives announcing that Gwen's brother is the new Duke of Shackerley, mother and daughter come up with a desperate plan: Gwendolyn will impersonate her brother and assume the dukedom until her brother can be located. But their confidence soon dwindles when the sinfully handsome Wickton meets them at the dock, and Gwen is hopelessly smitten.

A tale of love, deception, and the power of fate will entangle a desperate viscount with a daring female. Can he forgive her charade, or will he snuff out the burning passion that rages in her heart?

Kiss the Scoundrel Farewell #11

Lady Margaret marries out of duty only to find herself in the center of a scandal. Her husband, Baron Drake, dies in a duel over another woman. With no children and no desire to be shackled again, Meg decides to enjoy life as men do. She will be the other woman instead of the wife held captive by the whims of a man. Lady Drake enjoys the freedom of her widow's status.

Simon, Lord Hayward, a dutiful son with no fantasies of love, agrees to marry a wealthy heiress to plump the family's coffers. His father, in love with his mistress for decades, sets out to find his son one of his own. Simon scoffs at the idea, but when he meets an alluring courtesan at a masquerade, he finds himself smitten.

In a twist of fate, the masks come off, and Simon and Meg realize they met years ago, sharing a kiss in a duke's garden. Their secrets come out: She is no courtesan, and he is betrothed. After the viscount confesses his love, the baroness flees for the safety of the countryside.

As Lady Drake begins to doubt her scheme of being a paramour, Lord Hayward wonders if he can be happy with a wife who is not Meg and searches her out. He seeks her out only to find danger lurking in the idyllic English hills, and they soon learn the past has consequences no matter who you pretend to be.

Paddy's Peelers Mystery series

Set in the hectic district of Cheapside during the Regency, Paddy's Peelers search the dregs of London with skill and cunning to bring criminals to justice and, perhaps, unexpectedly find love along the way. A sweet but action-packed romance.

Crime, Conspiracies, and Courtship #1

Lady Matilda has always been an introvert, preferring her books to awkward conversations with strangers. As her first Season arrives, her mother insists she put away her bluestocking and concentrate on finding a husband. But Mattie is terrified of finding herself betrothed or even worse— not betrothed. The arrogant men of the ton terrify her.

Mr. Harry Walters is an orphaned, ex-Bow Street runner turned investigator, who makes a living by his wits. Working for Paddy O'Brien and his Peelers, often taking assignments for the Home Office, Walters is used to working closely with the beau monde. When a peer approaches him about a new assignment, Harry realizes they are both after the same man. He accepts the job but soon finds himself also protecting the earl's sister.

While working in costume at a masquerade, Walters makes a fatal mistake when he asks Lady Matilda to dance. It takes only a few stolen glances and one waltz for two unlikely souls to become hopelessly entwined. Mattie is determined to win the heart of this handsome, rugged man. Harry is just as determined to keep her safe.

Will fate find a way to bring a common man and an earl's sister a happy ever after? Or will his lack of title and dangerous life keep her at arm's length?

Pads, Purses, and Plum Pudding #2

Dr. Sampson Brooks is on a case that has nothing to do with medicine. He vows to help bring down the man who ruined his father and sent his mother to an early grave. When the villain's top henchmen are apprehended, Sam attends the hanging. While closing one chapter of his story, he unexpectedly opens another.

Dottie Brown, young and naïve, is duped by a charming swindler. A year after the wedding, she learns he's not what he pretends to be. Watching him on the gallows, she vows never to be taken in by romantic notions again. Yet fate tosses two obstacles in her path that day—a handsome physician and an abandoned child.

A chance encounter reveals one woman's secret, another man's revenge, and a love that will change their lives forever.

Poisons, Potions, and Parasols #3

She's content with her life…

Miss Eugenia Chapelle was born on the wrong side of the blanket. After her mother was disowned and fled to London, she pretended to be the widow of a French aristocrat to draw customers as a modiste. After her mother's death, Genie continues the lie, playing the half-French designer of Madame Chapelle's and running the business with her aunt. She never expects an earl to search out his illegitimate daughter twenty-six years later.

He will rip it apart…

Mr. Clayton Pierce works for one of London's most respected investigators. He has two cases on his docket—tracking a gang of counterfeiters passing banknotes and finding a long-lost child of an earl. When he meets the beautiful and talented Miss Chapelle, his attraction for her is as strong as his obsession with solving mysteries and catching criminals.

After Genie witnesses a possible murder at Hyde Park, she becomes a key witness in his first case. Then, by a twist of fate, she also becomes linked to his second assignment. With danger lurking around every dark corner, and the past the murkiest shadow of all, Clayton learns that solving a case does not always guarantee satisfaction of a job well done. As passions flare and the stakes are raised, will his success as an investigator be his ruin in love?

A MacNaughton Castle Romance series

Highland Regencies

"Witty and sensual!" Verified Purchase Review

"Lovely characters and complicated family conflicts. You will easily get caught up in their lives." Goodreads Review

A Merry MacNaughton Mishap (Prequel)

Rone finalist, InD'tale Magazine, N.N. Light Book Heaven finalist

Two feuding clans, one accidental encounter, a wee bit of holiday enchantment...

When Calum MacNaughton rescues a rival clan member from an icy drowning, he is unexpectedly rewarded with the clansman's most precious possession. Now Calum has until Twelfth Night to convince her to stay.

Deception and Desire #1

Nominated for Rone award, InD'tale Magazine, N.N. Light Book Heaven award winner

Two rebellious souls... An innocent deception... One scorching catastrophe...

Fenella Franklin's talents lie in numbers and a keen business mind, not in the art of flirtation. Lachlan MacNaughton has neither the temperament nor the patience to be the next MacNaughton chief, preferring to knock heads together rather than placate bickering clansmen. Their attraction sparks a passion they cannot deny. But will an innocent deception test their newfound love?

Allusive Love #2

A woman in love... An infuriating Scot... A tantalizing chase.

Kirstine has loved Brodie MacNaughton forever, but he considers Kirsty his best friend. When he turns to her for advice, she surprises him with an unexpected kiss that sends fire through his veins. When pride, Highland politics, and tragedy collide, he realizes how precious and allusive true love can be.

A Bonny Pretender #3

She's pretending to be someone she's not... His entire life is based on a lie...

Brigid MacNaughton becomes the perfect lady to placate her family, then falls in love with a quiet, self-possessed Englishman. Lord Raines is smitten with the beguiling and demure Scot. If he divulges his scandalous parentage, will she still fall willingly into his arms? Bonny pretender vs handsome imposter… Can love overcome a double deception?

A Medieval Encounter Series

Rolf's Quest

Great Expectations winner, Fire & Ice, Maggie finalist

"Romance, destiny, family values & betrayal all played parts in this intriguing novel that had me turning each page in anticipation."

The BookTweeter

A wizard, a curse, a fated love...

When Rolf finally discovers the woman who can end the curse that has plagued his family for centuries, she is already betrothed. Time is running out for the royal wizard of King Henry II. If he cannot find true love without the use of sorcery, the magic will die for future generations.

Melissa is intrigued by the mystical, handsome man who haunts her by night and tempts her by day. His bizarre tale of Merlin, enchantments, and finding genuine love has her questioning his sanity and her heart.

From the moment Melissa stepped from his dreams and into his arms, Rolf knew she was his destiny. Now, he will battle against time, a powerful duke, and call on the gods to save her.

Saving Grace (A Small Town Romance)

Contemporary and Colonial America

Holt and Maggie finalist

This unique piece has the reader traveling between the early 1700s and the early 2000s with ease and amazement. The audience truly feels sorrow for Grace and Chloe and is able to connect with each woman for the hardships they are overcoming... The attention to historical facts and details leave one breathless, especially upon learning the people from the past did exist and the memorial erected still stands. InD'tale Magazine

A tortured soul meets a shattered heart...

Chloe Hicks' life consisted of an egocentric ex-husband, a pile of bills, and an equine business in foreclosure until a fire destroys the stable and her beloved ranch horse. After the marshal suspects arson, she escapes the accusing eyes of her hometown.

Jackson Hahn, the local historian, distracts Chloe with a 17th-century legend of a woman wrongly accused of witchcraft. It might explain the ghostly happenings on the property. She is drawn to the similarities that plagued both their lives. Perhaps the past can help heal the present. But danger lurks in the shadows...

www.ingramcontent.com/pod-product-compliance
Lightning Source LLC
Chambersburg PA
CBHW020137180626
46810CB00004B/1596